Home Is Where
the Murder Is

Carolyn Rogers

An Imprint of
The Overmountain Press
JOHNSON CITY, TENNESSEE

Hardcover ISBN 1-57072-207-2
Trade Paper ISBN 1-57072-208-0
Copyright © 2002 by Carolyn Rogers
Printed in the United States of America
All Rights Reserved

1 2 3 4 5 6 7 8 9 0

In memory of Elizabeth Cox, who always believed. This one's for you, Mom.

A special thanks to my dad, Robert Cox, and my sisters, Robyn and Leslie, who shared their love of books with me, and to my wonderful husband, Kelly Rogers, my daughter, Tiffany, my son, Kelly, and my mother-in-law, Ruth Rogers, for always being ready with a hug of encouragement when I needed it most. I love you all.

Acknowledgments

So many people have helped me along the way to seeing my first mystery in print that to name each would take up at least five pages of text. I would, however, be remiss if I did not individually mention Tammie Schmid-Thompson, the best conference bud ever, Peggy Ramsey for coaching me through my first attempts at writing, Karen Syed and Diana Brandmeyer for commiserating with me over plot problems and uncooperative characters, and Debra Lee Brown and Sherri Browning for reminding me to *Focus, Carolyn, Focus!* when I needed it most.

Also, a special thanks to Julie Wray Herman for her cheerful guidance through the maze all new authors must travel. You kept me sane by leading the way. Thank you, Alison Hart, for teaching me more about the craft of writing than I ever found in any writing how-to manual, and for warning me about the perils of Doubter's Street. Whenever I insisted on visiting that dark place, you always made sure I was never alone. And, Lynda Mikulski, Wendy Ferguson, and Cheryl Johnson, mere thanks are not enough for always being there to share the joys and frustrations that come with bringing our stories to life. I honestly don't know what I'd do without you. I can't forget The Wild Ones, either—I was the last of the group to get published, but you let me stay anyway. Thanks for all the fun times we've had since we first met in cyberspace. And lastly, I must mention my good friends with the Aspiring Writer's Club—you guys have been with me since I created my first character so many years ago.

I am fortunate to know you all.

Chapter 1

I SWUNG MY LEG in its cumbersome brace out of the airport shuttle and hesitated, reluctant to step off into the well-known. Though only a few hundred mesquite-lined feet stretched between the van and my grandfather's guest ranch, from my vantage point it might as well have been a hundred miles. I wish it'd been about four times that and my daughter and I were safely back in San Antonio.

But that was the problem. I could no longer consider San Antonio safe.

The day I turned 18, Granddad told me, "Rachael, honey, if ever you get yourself into trouble, you can always come back home."

I guess I never believed I'd take up his offer. I'd spent too many years in the blistering-hot border town, scratching and clawing to get out. Why go back? Saddle Gap wasn't home. It was the place I'd spent my teenage years. That's all.

But thanks to Julio "The Flash" Fernando, I'd been forced to reconsider my way of thinking.

At least temporarily.

I shifted on the vinyl seat and reached for my crutches. The van's back door slid open and shut, jarring my damaged knee. I fought the urge to scream. Instead, I had to content myself with a strangled cry through clenched teeth.

Oblivious to my distress, my beloved daughter danced on the dirt road, kicking up a dusty storm. "Come on, Mom. Hurry."

"Hang on, kid. I'm moving as fast as I can."

Lauren flashed me her best impatient look: arms crossed, foot tapping, eyebrows furrowed. "You know, someone could have met us," she pointed out, not for the first time.

"And I told you, that's the last thing I need."

Maybe Lauren was right. We should have let someone know we were coming. But then if I had, Granddad would've insisted I stay at the ranch. I had no wish to impose on him, much less put myself in reach of all the mothering hens in my family.

A sobering vision crowded into my mind: I could see me, leg propped up on a stack of pillows, surrounded by steaming bowls of tortilla soup and towering plates of cabbage and spicy, meat-stuffed *gorditas*, while Carmita and her friends clucked at me to eat, eat, eat. I groaned at the thought. I was here to recover from my gunshot wound, after all. Not develop an ulcer.

"Ms. Grant, you need help getting out?"

I snapped back to reality. The driver's concerned gaze pushed me into action. Holding my crutches in one hand and bracing myself with the door handle, I peeled myself off the vinyl seat. I eased to a standing position, wincing at the little daggers of pain.

"No, I'm okay. I know you're in a hurry. You sure you don't mind dropping off our bags for us?"

The driver shook her head. "I run right by there on my way home. They'll be there by six."

"Okay, thanks."

"No problem."

I sighed. No problem? Sure, she'd drop the bags off where we were staying, but she couldn't take us down the hill to Tumbleweeds' main lodge. But I didn't want to complain. She'd already gone away from her route to take us this far from town. And like Lauren said, it really wasn't that much farther. Just down a rocky hill and through a long, endless dirt-and-gravel parking lot.

I could navigate that. I hoped.

With a honk of her horn and a friendly wave, our driver took off down the deserted road, leaving Lauren and me alone. I felt a sharp stab of unease as I watched the van turn onto the main highway and head toward town.

"Well, there's no turning back now, Mom."

"I suppose not."

I willed the van to stop, but it ignored my silent plea. Oh, well. At least, so far, the weather was cooperating.

I glanced at the clouds tumbling toward us, the shadows they cast creeping over land that seldom got much relief. I hoped today that the clouds were full of empty threats.

"Come on, kid. With my luck we'll get halfway down the hill and the sky will split wide open." I adjusted my fanny pack, comforted by the hard presence of my 9mm Glock. Rattlesnakes were common in these parts, and getting bit by one only five feet from Tumbleweeds was definitely not on the day's agenda. I hate snakes.

We headed down the road, Lauren a few watchful steps behind me. I swear, each step I took, a rock scuttled into my path, determined to trip me as we trundled down the hill. I still wasn't adept at navigating on my crutches. Lauren knew it. Those rocks certainly knew it.

"Only a few hundred feet, only a few hundred feet," I chanted beneath my breath. I could do this. It was no harder than chasing fleet-footed thieves while wearing cowboy boots.

Lauren abruptly stopped. "Wait, Mom."

I stopped, reaching for my gun. "What's wrong, pumpkin?"

"Look. It's beautiful," she said, her face suffused with pleasure. "So beautiful."

I looked up. Though I'd stood at this same spot hundreds of times, I couldn't help but appreciate her awe. Granddad always said, "Rachael, honey, no view on the Good Lord's earth is as fine as this one we got here."

At this moment, I believed he was right.

From where we stood we could see the dark waters of the Rio Grande through breaks in the surrounding ochre canyon walls. Shafts of sunlight pierced through the darkening clouds overhead and glimmered on the river's surface. Boulders I'd once clambered on littered the landscape, keeping company next to giant dagger yucca. A prairie falcon winked into existence, chasing some unseen prey. Close at hand, turkey vultures soared on wind currents, patiently waiting their turn at a kill.

I shuddered. I hate turkey vultures almost as much as I hate snakes.

It had been a while since I'd dared to breathe deeply, but I did so now, savoring the rare smell of coming rain. At home, on my beat, the smells of hot cement and molding trash are the most prevalent.

My work as a police officer on San Antonio's south side is tough, demanding, and, at times, ugly. Yet, despite the beauty before me, I ached to be back there, back to normalcy, back on the streets.

Tumbleweeds itself—made up of a main lodge, twelve cabins, stables, and a swimming pool—hadn't really changed much since my last visit; a little dustier, a little more worn. Otherwise, everything looked about the same. It was usually a busy place, but today seemed busier than normal.

I frowned at all the cars and vans jamming the parking lot. Then I noticed something. A cluster of beat-up, hubcap-less trucks with out-of-date inspection stickers was a dead give-away; my relatives were out in force.

"Are you sure you didn't tell Granddad we were coming?"

Lauren's face turned a delicate pink. "Well. . . ."

"Lauren Elizabeth!"

She sighed dramatically. "Just Daddy. He was the only one I told. Honest."

The ex. I hadn't planned on seeing Marshall, at least not right after arriving.

"Why didn't you warn me?" I demanded.

She paused. "I was afraid you wouldn't let us come."

I grimaced, though not from the pain. Normally she would have been right. But not this time. I smiled and jerked my head toward the lodge. "Go on, you imp. I'll catch up eventually."

She grinned and took off for the sidewalk. I hobbled after her, glad to see her enthusiasm return. The last few weeks had been tough on her. Lauren is a cop's kid. She understands the danger I face and handles it well.

Still, it wasn't every day her mom got shot. And what had come after my encounter with Fernando made my trouper of a child more skittish than a newborn filly. Not until I announced my plans to come to Saddle Gap for a while did I see the worry begin to smooth from her face.

We'd been right to come here.

I hoped.

Yet, I couldn't seem to shake the feeling of foreboding that had been with me since boarding the plane that morning.

"Mom, watch out!"

I glanced over my shoulder. A blue Bronco with dark, tinted windows roared toward me. There was no time to wonder where it had come from. I hurled myself between two cars as the vehicle jerked to the left and shot past me in a cloud of choking red dust and rocks.

Too close. Too close.

Lauren flew off the sidewalk and flung herself into my embrace, wrapping her thin arms around my waist. As I fought to regain my breath, I watched helplessly as the Bronco crested the hill and disappeared.

Damn. I didn't see the license number, didn't see anything at all. I stomped my crutches on the rocky road. Had only a few weeks away from patrol already stripped me of all my instincts?

"Mommy, who was that?"

"I don't know."

"It headed right for you!"

We both stared up the hill, but no answers came. Lauren trembled in my arms. I fought to regain my own composure.

"They probably just didn't see me. C'mon. I bet Carmita has something good to munch on. I'm starved."

Lauren's shoulders slumped. She nodded, but it was a reluctant motion. I could see the question she'd not asked of me, hiding within deep blue eyes so like her father's. *Are we safe here?*

I honestly didn't know.

But I wasn't about to tell Lauren that. I peeled myself from her death grip. The easiest way to distract her was to brave the masses inside Tumbleweeds.

Besides, what if the Bronco came back? I would be on the lookout, but I didn't want to see it again. Not yet.

"C'mon, munchkin. Don't worry about it."

She opened her mouth to protest, but I raised my hand and said, "And that's an order. Now scoot."

Spurred on by our encounter, Lauren ran up the sidewalk to the bottom of the steps and back again, a frantic puppy trying to hurry me up.

I hobbled up the stairs and pushed the door open with a crutch, wincing at the door's heaviness. Suddenly it pulled away and I stumbled. Disembodied hands grabbed for me, pulling me up before I could hit the floor.

"Oh, great," I mumbled against a broad chest. "Hi, Marshall." I immediately pulled back, but my ex held on, steadying me.

"Easy, Rachael. Sorry about that."

"No problem." My cheeks heated as whoops and welcomes sounded from every corner of the jam-packed room.

"You okay?"

I nodded.

Marshall peered at me from beneath his cowboy hat and released me, though I saw the doubt on his face, the worry in his eyes. Great. Lauren must have told him why we were coming.

Before he could say anything, I let other hands move me deeper into the crowd. From a safe distance I watched as Lauren bounded to her daddy and he swung her around in joy.

The old familiar hurt came back in force. I turned away, trying to focus on those welcoming me, trying not to watch as Lauren cuddled happily in her father's arms.

Here, she felt safe.

Marshall and I had never said much to each other throughout the years, ever since the day I learned Lauren was on her way. I was 18, and we had been married only a few months. The last thing I expected when I tracked him down in his daddy's barn to share my news was to discover he'd learned an ingenious new way to fork hay. With my best friend Pamela, I might add. I'll never forget the image of his bare backside, shining in the light from the open barn door.

I left him, and Saddle Gap, the next day. But now I was back for another visit.

Out of nowhere, what was left of my energy—after the long walk through the parking lot and the Bronco encounter—

suddenly disappeared. Everything and everyone around me started to shimmer, like a mirage on a hot desert road.

Granddad appeared out of nowhere. "She's going down! Quick, grab her something to sit on."

I felt myself eased onto a plastic-covered, gingham-checked bar stool. My leg was gently placed onto a chair's soft cushion. Someone shoved a beer in my hand.

With a stern grumble, Granddad replaced it with an ice-cold Vernors ginger ale. "She's on drugs, you know."

"Granddad!" Lauren chided as she walked up and gave him a bear hug. "They're prescription."

His eyes twinkled. "I was out back, bringing in some ice. Shoulda told me you was coming."

I glared at Lauren. "I thought you knew."

Granddad raised his gaze to the beamed ceiling and scratched his head. "Well, she mentioned somethin' about y'all maybe comin' down this way sometime or other."

Before I could argue further, my cousin Hogey and his wife, Cathy—who has far more patience than I would with the man—found me. Hogey's two buddies, beer cans in hand, trailed behind. Marvelous.

"Don't jostle her none now, Hogey," Cathy admonished as she peered at my leg. "That leg must hurt somethin' fierce."

But it was too late. He kicked the chair. Little cartwheels of sizzling pain catapulted up and down my leg, making my head spin.

"Dang it, Hogey, now look what you did," Cathy said. "Say you're sorry."

Hogey bowed his head. "Sorry, Rachael."

"Apology accepted," I said through gritted teeth as Cathy patted me on the shoulder.

Then the questions came in a dizzying rush:

"How many screws in there? I'm betting three. Robby's betting five."

"How much knee you got left, Rachael?"

"Were you scared? I'da been scared."

"Whatcha gonna do if they don't catch 'im, Rachael?"

Hogey waited, shifting back and forth from foot to foot. Once a handsome young man, too many years of sideline football and six-packs had left him with a gut the size of Montana. His Grateful Dead T-shirt barely covered the upper half of the state.

He grinned as he realized all eyes were on him. "Saw a story like 'at on 'Cops.' You hearda 'Cops,' Rachael? You gonna ever be on 'Cops'?"

I stared at him. Was I really related to this guy?

Someone said, "Think he'll come after you here?"

My gaze swiveled to a face I didn't recognize at first. An elf-like man in too-new red and black Western clothes pushed his way to the front. His shiny tan boots matched the pate revealed when he popped off his dirt-free Stetson and gave me a quick bow.

Stanley Fletcher? I shook my head.

He must've mistaken the dismay on my face for confusion. His hand shot out and grabbed for mine, but I snatched it back. Using crutches had left my palms near raw. Besides, like most cops, I don't like shaking hands with just anybody. Especially without gloves.

"Don't you remember me?" he said, his voice sliding into a whine.

I bit back my annoyance. "Oh, yeah, I remember you, Stanley."

My only prior encounter with Stanley had been brief and years ago, but how could I forget a five-foot-two version of Howdy Doody? "Why are you here?"

"It's a celebration," he said, throwing his hands up. "I bought your granddaddy's guest ranch!"

I stared, first at him, then at Granddad. "What do you mean, you bought the ranch?"

The room immediately quieted. Lauren, emerging from the kitchen with a huge cinnamon roll in her hand, stared at me. I realized then I'd yelled the words.

"Y-yes. The papers were finalized yesterday."

My mouth working soundlessly, I gaped at Granddad. Finally, I spit out, "You didn't tell me," in a pitiful squeak.

"Maybe I should excuse myself," Stanley mumbled.

"Maybe you should," I snapped, finding my voice again.

He backed away, his gaze fixed on my hands. Must have

worried I packed a gun. Of course I did, but he didn't know that.

"Rachael, listen to me." Granddad smiled and kissed my forehead. "The Good Lord's granted me 64 years of good health. Time for me to move on, do a few other things I've been settin' aside."

"But you can't sell the ranch! This is. . . . This is. . . . You are this ranch!" I opened my mouth to protest further, but then I stopped. Granddad's eyes filled with sadness, and for the first time in years, I looked at him. I mean, really looked at him.

Once-vivid red hair had given way to silver. His shoulders were straight as ever, but wrinkles creased the corners of his faded blue eyes—from a lifetime of laughing, mixed with a fair dose of sorrow. His hands, once strong and bronzed, were cracked and worn by endless hours of hard work.

Granddad was getting old.

But still I persisted. "Why him, Granddad?"

He sighed. "Good money. Enough to retire on so's I can spend my last days comfortable, fishin' and such. For what days left the Good Lord will grant me. It's a good offer, and I don't have no one else to leave it to, anyway. And Stanley'll take on Hogey and the other hands as well."

His words smacked my mouth shut. *No one else to leave it to.* I felt my cheeks heat in shame. More than once he'd asked if I'd be interested in taking on the ranch. But newly badged, I'd always refused.

"I understand. I guess."

He beamed. "There you go. I told Carmita you would. So much to do, Rachael! So many places to go. And now I finally can. Starting tomorrow."

"Aren't you going to stay around a little while longer?" Oh, help me, now I was whining.

"I'll be back in a few days. The boys are planning a retirement party for me on Friday. Can't miss that, now, can I?"

"Then where are you going tomorrow?"

His laughter filled the room. "Skiing."

I, too, laughed, despite myself. Granddad on skis? No way. "You'll end up on crutches, keeping me company."

He winked, tapping his shirt pocket and the little spiral tucked inside. "Nah. That's not on my list of things to do."

"What else are you planning? Fishing? Painting?"

He shrugged. "Maybe. The point is, Rachael, now I can do whatever I want. Even go hunting. I may be the one to bag the King, you know."

The King is a white-tailed buck of awesome proportions, with an antler spread big enough to break all records from here to Oklahoma. In these parts, "I spotted the King!" didn't mean an Elvis sighting.

I grinned. "So, the legend lives on."

"Yes, ma'am, indeed it does. And I aim to be the one to put that legend on my table."

"I hope you do, Granddad. Although, by now he'd probably be kinda gamey tasting."

He chuckled, his blue eyes twinkling. "He'd taste better'n a T-bone to me." He patted my good knee. "Just relax. I'll warn all the folks not to bother you none." He leaned over and kissed me on the cheek. "I'll tell Carmita to fetch you a cinnamon roll, too."

My stomach instantly growled. "I'd walk a thousand miles on these blasted crutches for one of those things."

He left, the spring in his step returning. I watched him poke his head into the kitchen.

Why hadn't I realized he wanted out? That he longed to sit with his friends on beat-up couches on the river's edge, smoking forbidden cigars and drinking ice-cold beer while time drifted aimlessly by?

I suddenly felt happy for Granddad, glad that someone, even a person like Stanley Fletcher, wanted to preserve what Granddad had built. But, I had to admit, I still wasn't thrilled that the ranch was no longer in the family.

Sipping my Vernors, I leaned back in my chair to watch the crowd. A little twinge of guilt lodged in my stomach as my gaze settled on Lauren. Her face was animated, her eyes twinkled, and her blonde ponytail bounced as she hugged each person who greeted her in turn.

She was at home here.

Watching her as she moved through the crowd, talking

to these people, I realized the longer we stayed here the harder it would be to take her back to San Antonio. It might be best to stay just through her spring break—long enough for my fellow cops back home to find Fernando—then get the heck out of Saddle Gap.

Feeling better, I drained the last of my Vernors. A week should be enough time. We'd be out of here in no time.

Unfortunately, Mr. Fletcher put an effective end to that idea the very next day.

Chapter 2

"MOM! WHERE ARE MY JEANS?"

I poked my head out from beneath my covers. My nice, warm, and cozy covers. I didn't want to wake up. Waking meant feeling. I didn't want to feel. But it was too late; my knee had already begun to trumpet, "The pain, the pain!"

"Go away!" I mumbled, turtling back into darkness.

"You talking to me, Mom?"

Reluctantly I peered over the edge of the quilt. Lauren stood in the doorway, dressed except for bare legs and the Reeboks she held in one hand. "You can't go out like that," I said.

She rolled her eyes. "Who were you yelling at a minute ago?"

"I wasn't yelling. I was talking to my knee."

She frowned. "Because. . . ." Then her face brightened. "Painkillers?"

"Yes. Please. I need my Vicodan."

"You find my new jeans, I'll find your medicine."

"Deal. Drugs first, though. I can barely move." I rolled over in the bed and peered over the edge. Our suitcases, open to reveal their jumbled innards, sat on the gleaming wooden floor.

We'd been too tired, on arriving from Tumbleweeds the night before, to bother with them further. Now they were a mess, thanks to Lauren's frenzied search for nightgowns and toothbrushes.

I'd rented a small but beautifully quaint two-bedroom cabin, which stood right where a stream narrowed and poured into the Rio Grande. The owners of the cabin, a couple of lawyers who lived in Houston but flew over once a month for the fishing (among other things), had gone to the extreme to make the sheltered cabin as homey as possible.

I'd met Mac and Allen while testifying on a search-and-seizure case they were handling. I visited their offices to give a deposition. Cold, stark, sterile, the world they worked in was a jungle of aluminum piping and black lacquer. The only aberration in this modern nightmare was the defiant stuffed rainbow trout on the wall in the conference room. I immediately told them about Tumbleweeds and fishing on the Rio Grande.

My description brought them both running, and before I knew it, they'd become Granddad's part-time neighbors. I doubted anyone in the law firm knew about the secret hideaway, and I'd agreed to preserve their privacy.

Beamed ceilings vaulted overhead, sheltering the heavy golden oak furniture and the odd mixture of Indian, Southwestern, and Spanish decorations. Thick white flokati rugs covered the floors. Original art, crafted by local artists, graced the washed pine walls.

I could understand Mac's and Allen's enchantment with their home away from home; they'd made their own slice of heaven here.

My plans were to spend the week sitting on the tiny back porch, drinking coffee and staring at the bubbling stream while mesquite and cottonwoods waved overhead. This small, secluded cabin and its surroundings were soothing, healing to the mind and body. I intended to do that a lot over the next few days. Soothe and heal. And be as private as the mom of a 13 year old with an active social life can be.

"Hey, Mom. Jeans?"

I shook myself back to reality and riffled through the nearest suitcase, which happened to be Lauren's. I found at least five more shirts than I'd told her she could bring, but no jeans.

"Which suitcase did you pack them in?" I said, sitting up. Bending over made me dizzy.

"Your brown one."

I frowned as I realized—no brown suitcase. "It's not here."

A panic-stricken look crossed her face. "But I just got them!"

"Why weren't they in one of your own suitcases?"

"Not enough room. Oh, great. This is just great. What am I gonna do?"

I threw the covers back and eased off the bed, groping for my crutches. Hobbling into the bathroom, I listened as Lauren continued to grumble.

"This is just great. It figures. It just figures."

"Wear your white jeans," I suggested.

"But they'll get dirty! Dad's taking me horseback riding!"

I grabbed a bottle of Tylenol, shaking out two. Then two more. I'd find my Vicodan later. "Wear the ones you had on last night." *God, please grant me patience*, I prayed, as a plaintive wail issued from my room.

"But I can't wear them again! Everyone saw me in them yesterday! I'd rather die!"

I slammed the medicine cabinet shut. "Geez, Lauren, when I was your age, I wore the same jeans for a week at a time. Proudly. Why, they could practically stand up by themselves."

She poked her head into the bathroom, her nose wrinkled. "That's gross, Mom. Really gross."

"Go put them on."

She opened her mouth, but I think my glare must have been extra-intimidating. She nodded and slithered away.

Satisfied, I left the bathroom and plopped down on the bed. "I'll have to call the airport shuttle later and see if they found it."

Lauren bounded up to me and smacked me on the cheek. "That's okay. It was mostly your stuff, anyway." All smiles, she tore out of the room. What a roller coaster.

Then it hit me. My Vicodan was in that suitcase. Great. Before I could find the energy to budge again, a car honked out front.

"Bye, Mom! See you later!" The door slammed shut before I could react.

"Love you, too," I mumbled to the empty room. But I was secretly glad Lauren had run out to meet Marshall. What if he'd come to the door? I was a mess. Really ugly. And bound to get uglier before the day was over; in a scant thirty minutes, my ex's sister, Jamie, would be by to take me to physical therapy and torture session number one. I could hardly wait.

* * *

I had spent about twenty minutes in a more or less successful attempt to wash my hair—my blistered palms stinging and thus making it a near impossible task—when the doorbell rang. I froze. I was, after all, sitting naked in the bathroom on the toilet, my hair sopping wet. My crutches were in the bedroom, leaning on the bed.

"Hold on!" I hollered, hopping to the sink and grabbing a towel. I quickly wrapped it around my body, fighting the shivers. Man, the floor was cold. A quick glance at my hair in the mirror over the sink made me frown. Bubbles. Darn it.

The doorbell rang again.

"Hold on a minute," I hollered louder. I tried to wrap another towel around my head, but I was standing on one good leg while the other pounded in rhythmic protest, so I gave up.

I finally managed to get my crutches and hobble through the kitchen and halfway to the door when Jamie burst inside, nearly making me lose my towel.

"How'd you get in?" I said, startled.

"Door was unlocked." She contemplated me and shook her head. "Geez, Rachael, you look like hell."

I smirked. "Thanks."

At first glance Jamie looked terrific. Her hair, sandy blonde like her brother's, was pulled up into a ponytail, making her look even younger than she was. Her eyes shone with good humor. She had on a pair of black-and-purple tennis shoes and a T-shirt over black exercise leotards. But then I took note of the circles beneath her eyes, the paleness of her skin. Unusual for Jamie.

At that moment, my precariously wrapped clothing chose to unwrap, so I didn't have time to speculate about her condition. I grabbed futilely for the towel.

Jamie smirked and bounced to the refrigerator, sticking her head inside. "No Vernors? Oh, and good thing I wasn't my brother," she said.

"He's already been here. Took Lauren horseback riding this morning."

She winked. "He's been doing that a lot lately. 'Specially after hearing you were coming."

"Jamie."

She peered at me innocently beneath her bangs. "Yes, dear?"

"Shut up."

She laughed and gestured toward my head. "I like the bubbles."

I reached up and ran my hand through my hair. "You ever tried to wash your hair with only one leg to stand on?"

"No, can't say as I have, Rachael. C'mon. Lean over the kitchen sink, and I'll rinse it for you."

As Jamie enthusiastically drenched my hair, I clutched the counter and my towel. She turned the water to almost scalding, but it felt good. Incredibly good, especially when she added some conditioner and her strong hands began to massage my scalp. Knowing I was in for some serious torture later, the magical moments of pampering were very much appreciated.

She knew what she was doing. Jamie and Marshall's mom once owned and operated one of the Gap's favorite beauty shops. When I first arrived in Saddle Gap to live with my grandparents, my grandmother took me immediately to Emma's Hair Affair for the "Ultimate Treatment." I still remember that day, the first time I began to feel loved again.

Of course, the Hair Affair was now closed. Emma, now a widow, had been undergoing chemotherapy for breast cancer and had been forced to close her shop. Jamie had taken time off from school to care for her mother.

"You know, your hair would look a lot better if you'd whack it off." She scrubbed my head vigorously, massaging the back of my neck. I could have purred, it felt so good. "At about your shoulders."

"But then I couldn't pull it back into a ponytail," I shouted over the running water.

"You shouldn't do that," she said. "It's bad for your hair to keep it up all the time. Not that I don't do the same thing."

"Can't exactly chase bad guys with hair flying in my face."

She laughed. "What you need is a good haircut. Next time I come over I'll do it, if you want me to." She started to rinse my hair. "Get rid of this gray, too."

"Okay, I'll think about it. Oh, hey. How's your mom?"

Jamie stopped spraying my hair. "What?"

"Your mom. How is she?" I closed my eyes as she brought my head up with a quick snap. "Hey, easy there."

"Sorry. Here's a towel." I reached out blindly, but she had already attacked my head, drying it enthusiastically. "Not so good. Chemo's pretty darn rough, but the last few days she's felt a bit better."

"I'm sorry, Jamie."

"Yeah. Well, them's the breaks."

I took the towel from Jamie and peered at her in surprise, but she turned away and walked to the living area. I shrugged and headed for my room to change.

My own parents' deaths had been quick and, as far as I knew, relatively painless. Grandmother's illness had kept her lingering for a short while, but I was long gone from Saddle Gap by then.

I felt for Jamie, but I didn't know what to say. The usual platitudes seemed trite and uncaring. I'd think of something to do for her later, though. Maybe help with Emma, give Jamie a break. "I'll be ready in a minute."

"Okey dokey. Sure you don't need help?"

"Nope. Thanks."

"Guess who else is in town?" she said suddenly, pushing herself to the edge of the couch. "You won't believe it."

I paused in my doorway, still awkwardly holding onto my towel. "Who?"

Her eyes glistened as she grinned an evil, mischievous grin. "Your former best friend. Ms. Pamela Pianka herself. Can you believe it? What are you going to do?"

"Okay, Lieutenant. Let's see some action!"

"But it hurts, dammit!" I glared at Malik with my best mom look, but unlike my daughter, he refused to cower. He'd known me too long, I guess, to be intimated—first as a friend, and now as my physical therapist/torturer. I think he enjoyed his newest role in my life a bit too much. "My Vicodan was in that suitcase."

"What suitcase?"

"One of my suitcases is missing. I told you that already," I said, feeling highly annoyed. "It had my Vicodan in it."

He shook his head at me. "You don't need that stuff anymore, anyway. I thought cops were tough. Look at you. A five year old could do better. Get mad!"

"I am, dammit!" Oh, boy, was I. I couldn't believe Pamela was back. Pamela, who had left Saddle Gap soon after I did, though I doubted it was in shame for what she'd done with my husband.

"Lift that leg. Again! C'mon, Lieutenant!"

"My name is Rachael," I spit out between clenched teeth.

"Then don't call me Dammit."

I fell back against the mat. My heart pounded. Sweat poured into my eyes. I was hungry. "I don't like you."

"You'll *hate* me before this session is over. Now come on, Rachael. Lift that leg!"

I closed my eyes and obeyed. Unfortunately, the ever-present image of my nemesis plugged into my mind with my spouse.

Ex-spouse.

My eyes shot open. I had no idea what I was going to do about this new situation. I wasn't in the mood for Pamela. I wasn't in the mood for Marshall, either, when it came right down to it. I'd been through enough misery lately.

And now I was going to go through even more. I couldn't believe it—mere weeks after surgery to remove two slugs from my kneecap, and I was doing leg lifts.

And Malik was right—I was beginning to hate him. But I could tell he wasn't worried. He never did take me seriously.

"Stop daydreaming, Mrs. Grant."

"That's *Ms.* Grant," I spit out between curses.

Assorted grunts, groans, and whines filled the room as victims of various mishaps slammed, pushed, and threw themselves through prescribed routines.

Weights clanged, machines slammed about. Wheels whirled as those on stationary bicycles—myself included—fought up imaginary hills in pursuit of wellness.

It was one hellacious hour.

I had just settled my screaming knee into a blissfully bubbly and hot whirlpool, a glass of Gatorade in my hand, when Lauren burst into the room. A very white-faced, frightened Lauren.

"Mom! Oh, Mom. . . ."

I nearly jumped off the platform around the tub. Malik's strong hand pushed me back down, or I would have ended up splattered on the floor.

"Lauren, what's wrong?" I said. "Where's your dad?"

"Right here. Rachael, we need to talk."

I glared at Marshall, then focused on Lauren. There were no signs of bruises or bleeding. "What happened—"

"Nothing happened." Marshall glanced at Malik. "I need to talk to Rachael for a moment. Would you mind showing Lauren where she can get a drink?"

"Why, sure. C'mon, Lauren. Drinks are on me."

I squeezed her hand. "Go on, honey. Your daddy will tell me what's going on."

She nodded but I could sense her reluctance to leave, though she did so without argument. Malik glanced over his shoulder as he started to follow her, the "you okay?" question hovering in his eyes. I nodded once. He frowned at Marshall's back, then left, closing the door behind him.

Oblivious as always, Marshall went on. "Something's happened. I don't know how to tell you."

I smirked. "I'm a big girl, Marshall. Spill it."

Instead of getting angry, he sat down next to me. There was just enough room for two. To my surprise, he picked up my hand—the one that once wore the cheap diamond chip he'd given me. I admit it, I'm the sentimental sort about some things—I saved the ring for Lauren. But he didn't know that.

He rubbed his thumb across my knuckles once and then, as if belatedly realizing what he was doing, let my hand go. He stood and turned his back to me, then immediately turned around, his face clouded with horror and concern. It's obvious whose genes gave Lauren her penchant for drama.

"Stanley Fletcher was just found at Tumbleweeds."

I shrugged. "He's buying it from Granddad. So?"

"He's dead, Rachael. Two fishermen found him there, hanging upside down from the back porch."

Chapter 3

I STARED AT MARSHALL in disbelief. "What do you mean?"

His expression hardened. "Stanley's dead, Rachael. He looked like a fresh-kilt deer, all trussed up and swinging back and forth in the breeze. I'm sorry, but Lauren saw him. Only for a second, though," he added.

I snapped my head back, eyes closed. How dare he expose our daughter to that? Biting back the slashing remark I wanted to hurl at him, I said, "Tell me what happened."

Marshall sat down and dropped his head into his hands. When he spoke, I could barely understand his mumbling. "Lauren and I were headed toward the stables. We'd gone to McDonald's for breakfast."

"Geez, Marshall. She's not six anymore."

"It was her suggestion," he snapped, raising his head.

I bit my tongue. "Go on."

He ruffled his hand through his hair. Sweat beaded his brow, and his face was a peculiar pinkish-gray beneath his tan. As he spoke, his natural color slowly returned. "We'd just driven up to the turnoff to Tumbleweeds, when two fishermen flagged us down. Said they'd seen someone they thought was dead."

"Who were they? Anyone I know?"

"Curt and Robbie Conard."

I shook my head. "Very credible witnesses," I said sarcastically. Curt and Robbie were brothers and experts at brewing blackberry wine. And buddies of my cousin Hogey. Bottles of their hooch filled the rundown shack of a house they inhabited. I'd gotten drunk on the stuff myself more than once—thanks to Hogey. They stayed drunk on it constantly, living on it and whatever fish they could yank out of the Rio Grande.

Marshall snorted. He obviously agreed with my assessment. "We went back down to Tumbleweeds—"

"You didn't let them in your car, did you?" I asked, horrified at the thought.

He scowled. "Heck, no. They walked. We drove down the hill to Tumbleweeds and parked." He spread his hands, his expression returned to sober. "I told Lauren to wait in the car in the parking lot. She came after us anyway. I swear, I didn't know she'd do that. I wouldn't have taken her down there if I'd known."

I took a deep breath and pushed myself to a stand. "Where is Stanley now?"

"Still there. The sheriff wanted me to fetch you and take you down there."

I'd already hopped for the door before he got halfway through his sentence. After grabbing my crutches and arranging for Malik to watch Lauren, I headed straight for Marshall's red Jeep. I hauled myself in, buckled up, and glared straight ahead. "Hurry, Marshall."

He said nothing as he climbed into the Jeep and started it up. We headed away from the clinic and for the back roads, the quickest way to Tumbleweeds, past the foot of Side Saddle Plateau.

Saddle Gap lies northwest of Big Bend National Park, more than twenty miles from its nearest cosmopolitan neighbors, Marfa, Marathon, and Alpine. Nestled between two plateaus—Side Saddle Plateau and Saddle Horn Plateau—the small town never had much to boast about except for its proximity to the state park and the Rio Grande, and, of course, its excellent hunting. But now, with the first hints of warm spring air shooting between the plateaus, all sorts of folks had begun to converge on the Gap.

The twenty minutes it took to get to Tumbleweeds stretched out, passing slower than crossing the Sahara on crutches. Pickup trucks and station wagons, towing everything from beat-up kayaks to the most sophisticated fishing boats, crowded the highway. Not one, but four blue Broncos. Once again I felt a flare of anger for my sluggish reaction in the

Tumbleweeds parking lot.

In an effort to forget my own ineptitude, I studied the landscape while the Jeep hurled toward our destination, and I let my thoughts turn to other worries. I had no idea if Tumbleweeds was actually still Granddad's or not, and the distress which comes from not knowing fueled my frustration.

The implications of Stanley's death were unknown, but I knew it was going to be a mess. A huge, horrid mess. Did he have any heirs? Did he even have time to make arrangements for all the "what-ifs" that came along with owning a ranch?

The employees were on a short leave of absence—I knew that much. But it wouldn't last for long. Hot gossip traveled faster than a turkey vulture after road kill in desert country; within two hours, the employees would start trickling back, wondering what was to come of their jobs. Their entire lives.

I had no idea what to tell them.

"You okay?" Marshall asked.

Great. Didn't he know I didn't want to talk? I turned away from the window and glared at the biggest disappointment in my life, then broke my own silence. But even I was surprised at what came out. "Did you know Pamela is in town?"

The car swerved.

"Geez, Marshall! Watch it!"

"Sorry. Sorry." His hands gripped the wheel, knuckles white. He cleared his throat. "Yeah, I know. How'd you know?"

"Jamie told me."

He frowned, returning his attention to the road. "What did she say?"

I quelled my exasperation. "That Pamela was in town. That's all. I told her I didn't care."

His hands relaxed a little, I noted. I also noted he didn't offer a reply. I sighed in relief when we pulled up to the driveway in front of Tumbleweeds. Marshall eased his Jeep up to a deputy who stood guard at the entrance. The deputy crouched down, saw it was us, and waved us on.

The parking lot was jammed. The sheriff. An ambulance. The local news van. And an ominously large white car with the words COUNTY CORONER on the side. I didn't recognize the other cars.

The Conard brothers stood to one side, shoulders thrown back and hands waving, as they retold their story for the cameras aimed their way. I noticed that the reporters were standing a few extra feet back from the odiferous pair. One of the brothers gestured with his hands like he was being hung, and then he pointed toward Tumbleweeds.

"Stop the car."

"Rachael, they told me to have you wait in the parking lot until someone came to get you—"

I opened the car door, and he screeched to a stop. Several onlookers swiveled to look, but I didn't care. I grabbed my crutches and used one to slam the door, effectively cutting off Marshall's protests.

Although my last walk through this parking lot had been slow and halting, this one was rushed. I pushed my way past the good citizens, who were standing around openmouthed. Some were a distinct shade of green.

Stanley must be quite a sight. I hobbled past the stone benches and around the trees to the back, ignoring those who tried to stop me. I approached the crowd gathered around the back porch, ready to fight my way through, if necessary.

Stanley Fletcher was gone.

Someone touched my shoulder. "Excuse me. Mrs. Grant?"

I shrugged the hand off, and the deputy stepped back. "Where's the sheriff?" I asked him.

"He's making a statement, Mrs. Grant. If you'd like to follow me—"

I ignored him. Sheriff Rosa stood talking to a portly man stuffed into an impeccably tailored gray suit at least one size too small. The man spread his beefy hands wide as he talked, jowls flapping like a bulldog, about "the dire situation at hand." A camera caught every moment.

Tom Hall, with his best concerned look plastered on his face, glanced my way. I nodded once. His eyes bugged out in surprise, then he cast a quick glance toward the camera and hurriedly finished his speech. The camera turned toward me, but Sheriff Rosa blocked its view. The cameraman shrugged and trotted off after other prey.

"Where's the body, Sheriff?" I asked.

He smiled, a placating, well-practiced smile. "We already took him down, Rachael. Now, we couldn't let poor Mr. Fletcher hang up there any longer, could we?"

"Dammit, Sheriff, I would've liked to have seen him for myself."

The smile poured into a frown. "Now, Rachael, it wasn't something you'd want to see. Besides. You aren't part of this investigation." He shook his head back and forth, his brown eyes filled with sorrow. Sheriff Rosa reminded me of my dog, Higgins, an expert in the mournful look. It was hard to tell if the man was serious or not.

"I've seen far worse than a dead man hanging upside down, Sheriff. Where's the body?"

He gestured toward the ambulance, which had started to silently pull away. No reason to turn the sirens on for the dead. "The poor deceased is on his way to the county morgue."

"Why didn't you wait for me to get here?" Part of me wondered why I was overreacting, while the other wanted to scream.

The sheriff's face hardened. "Now, Rachael, we asked Marshall to fetch you to help us locate your grandfather. Not to help out here. It don't concern you."

I strove to regain my calm. "Granddad's not here, Sheriff, so it, in fact, does concern me. I'll have to tell him everything that's been done here. Are there any witnesses?" I gestured toward the Conard brothers, where they lounged, smoking, against a police car. "Credible ones, I mean? Was the area photographed?" I looked around. People trampled everywhere. I was incredulous. "Dammit, Sheriff. What are all these people doing here?"

Not waiting for his answers, I pushed my way through the crowd of reporters, sheriff's department personnel, and onlookers, the sheriff following after me.

I couldn't believe the mayhem. Conducting a crime scene like this would have gotten someone fired back home. The expression on my face must have been something else, as the crowd parted like the waters did for Moses. I stopped, breathless, at the foot of the stairs leading to the back door.

Sheriff Rosa caught up with me. "Now, Rachael, hold on just a second here. We've taken care of what needs to be taken care of. We might not be as sophisticated as you big-city cops, but we know what we're doing."

I rubbed my hand across my face and sighed. I didn't want to make an enemy of this man—he was a good friend of my grandfather's, after all. "I'm sorry, Sheriff. I didn't exactly expect to find something like this when I decided to come back to Saddle Gap."

He smiled and patted me on my shoulder. "That's fine, Rachael. Your granddaddy went skiing, someone said. Is that true?"

"I don't know where, though, Sheriff."

"You find him, tell him to give me a call."

"I will."

"Take a look inside, Rachael, and see if anything looks out of place. Don't touch nothing, though."

I bit my tongue. "I won't. I promise."

He smiled, apparently well pleased I was behaving myself and would do as he said, like a good girl.

Frustrated with my crutches, I hopped up the stairs, using the railing for support. A small circle of crime-scene tape had been tied around lawn chairs, presumably where Stanley had hung. I closed my eyes in disbelief; then, as best I could, I knelt on my good knee.

Blotches of dried blood, blended with dirt, tromped up the stairs from the yard. I glanced overhead. No detectable marks made by the rope from where I knelt, but I knew closer examination would likely reveal marks in the cypress. Problem was, there was no way I could get up there. Not in my present condition.

I sat on my backside in disgust. I didn't even know what kind of rope it was he'd been hung with, and I doubted seriously anyone would volunteer to inform me.

"Excuse me, ma'am? Deputy Rittenour. Do you remember me?"

I looked up. Except for my new companion, I was alone

on the porch. He stood so that the sun shone over his shoulder, blinding me. I tried to stand, then realized, to my ever-growing frustration, I was stuck.

He hunkered down until we were eye to eye. Dressed in jeans worn almost white, a slightly wrinkled yellow tennis shirt, and holey Top-Siders, he certainly didn't look like any of the other deputies. He glanced at his attire and flashed me a lopsided grin. "Deputy Rittenour, retired, that is. I was sent in to help you out in here."

It was Nick, my friend Jenn's little brother, though a quick perusal proved he wasn't so little anymore. I held out my hand. He frowned for a moment, then realized what I wanted. He stood, pulling me up with him.

"Thanks. I don't think sitting down was a good idea."

"No, ma'am. Likely not." He flashed another grin.

"Retired?"

"Retired, as in one week from now, I'm off to Border Patrol Academy up in Georgia. I was out walking my dogs along the river when I heard the sirens." He ran one hand across a day's growth of beard and gestured toward the bloodstains. "I understand you have some questions. Rosa said to take good care of you."

I frowned. The last thing I needed was to be "taken care of," especially on the sheriff's orders. "More like make sure I behave myself, I imagine."

He laughed lightly. "Well, yes, ma'am, I suppose so."

Ma'am? I took a good look at Nicky Rittenour. Little Nicky, as Jenn always called him, had been one of those kids who'd always seemed to be underfoot, hanging around, trying to break into our secret gigglefests. A genuine pest. But he'd been a cute kid, Jenn's favorite of her four younger brothers. So, most of the time we'd let him hang around, along with the two or three dogs that usually tagged after him.

Today was no exception. An overgrown boxer nosed his way onto the porch, chuffing in excitement, followed by a slightly more sedate German shepherd. Last, a tiny dog, ugly as his companions were beautiful, followed on their heels. The little mutt sneezed once then plopped down on his belly. He laid his head between his paws but looked up, attentive to his buddies. The brush-like tail waved back and forth.

The boxer wiggled his way up to me, nearly knocking me down in his enthusiasm. Nick grabbed the dog's collar and pulled him back, then herded his crew back off the porch. He spoke sternly to the dogs, then leapt back up to join me on the porch.

"Sorry about that. You okay?"

"I'm fine. I have a dog myself."

His eyes lit up and he grinned, flashing perfect white teeth. "What kind?"

"A bearded collie."

"Did you bring him with you?"

I shook my head. "No, he's staying with a friend. We flew, and I couldn't see bringing him out for such a short visit. What are their names?"

"The boxer's name is Kachina. The little guy is Chili Dog."

"Chili Dog? Jenn name that one?"

Nick laughed. "You do remember me, then. Yeah, she named Chili Dog. The shepherd is Tor."

"He's beautiful." I paused, briefly at a loss as to what to say next. I finally gestured to the back door. "Are they done inside?"

"Yes, ma'am, I believe so."

"Ma'am?" I cocked my head at Nick. "I'm only about six years older than you, you know."

"Five, actually."

"Five, then. Just please don't call me *ma'am*, okay? *Rachael* is fine. How is Jenn, anyway? I haven't seen her in a while."

"Been in Mexico the last few days, on the hunt for the perfect pepper for this year's salsa contest."

"Sounds like Jenn. Her shop must be doing well."

"Very well. I've been pinch-hitting for her now that I'm unemployed. I understand you're a cop yourself."

I smiled. This was Saddle Gap, after all. Even if Jenn hadn't told him, I doubted he wasn't aware of that fact. "Yes. Just crossed ten years."

He nodded, his expression thoughtful. The same deputy who had tried to distract me before ran up to him. His gaze flicked to me and back to Nick. The deputy spoke urgently to Nick for a moment.

Nick glanced at me. "Excuse me for a second, Rachael. I'll be right back with you."

I nodded, but he'd already returned his attention to the deputy. I wondered what they were saying. I also didn't necessarily care for being left out.

"Thanks, Mike," he finally said, his voice drifting toward me.

Mike the deputy nodded and took off.

"Sorry about that," Nick said, returning to me.

"What was that about?"

He smiled humorlessly. "I'm sorry, I can't say."

"You won't tell me what he said?"

"Not at the moment, no. I can't."

Fine. I glanced up at Stanley's beam. I wondered how long I'd think of it that way—maybe forever. "Well, will you at least tell me what kind of rope was used?"

"We don't think the hanging was what necessarily killed him, ma'am. Rachael."

"How, then?"

"Someone thwacked an arrow into his chest."

I winced. "Like a deer."

Marshall had said Stanley was trussed up like a deer, but he'd said nothing about an arrow. And my daughter had seen that? Anger percolated, but there was nothing I could do about it now. Lauren knew I dealt with ugly stuff on a daily basis, but I always made sure to leave it back at the office, out on the streets. And I'd been successful until Fernando shot me—and before we came here.

"Yes," he said.

It took me a moment to refocus on our conversation. *Deer arrow. Right.* "What kind?"

"I don't know much about bow hunting. I was never interested in killing animals." He looked up, then glanced around. A pile of twisted nylon rope lay on the ground, the kind of rope a fisherman uses to tie stringers of fish to boats. "The rope was like that. Only heavier."

"Any idea how he was hoisted up there?"

"Yes, ma'am. Motorized boat winch."

Boat winch. Then size didn't necessarily matter. Stanley wasn't a big man, not by a long shot, but to hoist even a hundred pounds overhead without some sort of assistance would be tough for most people. With a boat winch, it would be a simple matter of tying up the person and punching a button.

I also knew, however, that Granddad kept his boat winches locked up during the winter months, along with the river rafts. It was almost time to bring them out, but not quite. "Nick, has anyone checked the boathouse?"

"Yes. It'd been broken into. And, yes," he added, "it's been gone over."

"Good. What about inside the main lodge?"

"They've already finished in there, if you'd like to take a quick look around."

"This door was unlocked? Or was it broken into, too?"

"Unlocked."

He pushed open the door and bounded inside, reminding me of his dogs. I followed with a bit less enthusiasm.

The back door opened into a private living area, which included a kitchen and a small living room complete with a cozy, bright red, overstuffed couch. Well-worn easy chairs flanked either side. This had been Granddad's territory; didn't matter what it looked like to him, though I had imagined Stanley would have tossed the chairs out first thing.

A wood-burning stove sat in the corner. It wasn't used often, but I could smell the lingering scent of mesquite, mixed with the ever-present cinnamon. Folks came from all over for Carmita's breakfast rolls.

I wondered what would happen to her now.

Nick watched, remaining silent, as I carefully examined the living area. Powder residue lightly covered every surface. It was going to be difficult getting it off everything. Nothing seemed disturbed, I didn't smell anything unusual, and nothing seemed out of place. No drinks spilled, no strange markings, no spatters of blood.

I peeked into the office. Everything in there seemed orderly as ever. Pictures of Lauren at various ages cluttered the desk, along with the usual desk paraphernalia. Stapler. Tin can full of pens and pencils. A tape dispenser.

An open Coke can sat on the desk. I was surprised it hadn't been taken in for examination. I'd have to mention it to the sheriff. There were also a couple of small stacks of numbered photographs from the Glory Wall. On top of one of the stacks was a picture of me, Marshall, and Jamie. The next one was of Pamela and me with Marshall and Jamie. Marshall crouched in front of us, holding the head up of his first kill of bow-hunting season, an eight-point buck with a terrific spread. He'd been so proud of that kill. I'd been sort of sick to my stomach, I remembered. I understand the rationale of keeping the deer population manageable in size, but I can't see the joy of killing off beautiful, living creatures.

I picked up the photograph, smiling at my own ill-disguised distaste, feeling the familiar smoldering disappointment as I studied Pamela's face proudly beaming over Marshall's shoulder. Even then, I suspected, she'd wanted Marshall. I tossed the photograph down, and it landed blank side up. Good. The less I saw of that woman the better.

A small folder marked INVOICES lay on the chair along with a giant ledger. Granddad had never made it to the computer age, still relying on handwritten records going back twenty years and more. I opened the folder and glanced through it—nothing out of the ordinary there, although I was surprised the folder hadn't been taken for examination. I shook my head.

"Anything seem off?" Nick asked.

"From what I can tell, nothing's out of place. Or missing. But I can't know for sure."

"Inventory?"

"I'll have to check with Granddad or Carmita for that." I looked at Nick. "Carmita. She should be here. Has she been seen around?"

"No. She has keys to the place?"

I hesitated. It was second nature to me to want to protect Carmita. Her family was somewhere in Mexico. Fifteen years earlier, Granddad met her in the Tumbleweeds parking lot. She had no money but sported two black eyes and a fistful of brand-new, top-of-the-line fishing vests she'd stolen from the Tumbleweeds gift shop.

Granddad was always ready to help a lost one in need. Instead of having her thrown in jail, he'd offered her a job, much to everyone's surprise. But his belief in her paid off. She'd been a staple at Tumbleweeds ever since.

Yet, trusting Granddad's judgment, I knew very little about her. I didn't even know how old she was. But I did know one thing. Carmita would never betray him by doing something like this.

"Carmita would never hurt anyone," I said. "I know she wouldn't."

Nick's dark eyes rested on mine for a moment. "How well do you know Carmita?"

"Well, I—"

"What's her last name?"

I looked at him in surprise. "I'm not sure."

"Where is she from?"

"She never really said, except from somewhere near Mexico City. She didn't like to talk about it, and I respected that." I caught Mr. Future Border Patrol's look. "And yes, she's legal."

"How did she feel about him selling the place?"

"I—" Darn. I had no idea. "I don't like being on this side of the questions," I said, sinking onto the couch. My knee hurt, my head felt fuzzy, and my burst of adrenaline-charged energy had suddenly depleted, dropping me into an abyss of exhaustion. I ducked my head into my hands and squeezed my eyes tight against the throbbing in my leg and in my head. I hurt. Oh, how I hurt. I couldn't think straight, either.

Nick waited for me to compose myself, not saying anything. When I finally looked up, I was surprised to see he was watching me. He sat on a small wooden stool, his head bent to the side a little, curiosity and compassion reflected in his eyes. He motioned to my leg. "Bad, isn't it."

I nodded. His gaze locked with mine, but I gave in first and looked away. I had to. Either that, or I would throw myself at him, which isn't like me at all—except, maybe, in my imagination. Where the sudden flash of pure lust came from, I had no idea. This was crazy. How could I be attracted to someone who, last time I had seen him, barely reached my chin?

But there it was. And darn it, he knew.

I should have stayed in San Antonio.

Pushing myself up, I hobbled over to the window. The parking lot had almost cleared, except for the sheriff, a few stragglers, and Marshall, who stood next to his Jeep, talking to one of the reporters. I wondered how many times he would manage to pitch his business's name during the interview. Annoyed, I turned from the window and leaned against the wall.

"Tell me about Carmita," Nick said.

I hesitated, then finally said, "Well, when Carmita first came and Granddad told me about her, I didn't pay much attention. She slid into life around here, picking up some of the things my grandmother used to do, in exchange for living here. She's a wonderful cook, and the kitchen is her domain. She's indispensable to Granddad."

Nick frowned. "Do you have any reason to believe they could have developed a relationship?"

I nearly laughed out loud. "No. Oh, no. My gosh, Granddad must be twenty years older than Carmita."

Nick shrugged. "Age doesn't matter. Where else could she be, do you know?"

"She's probably at Granddad's house. She'll know where he is."

"You don't?"

This time I was the one who shrugged. "It wasn't necessary for him to leave me the details of his trip." I glanced out the window at the yellow crime-scene tape. "At least, I thought not. Anything else?"

He stood. "Not for now. You're staying at Mac's place, right?"

"Yes."

"For how long?"

I searched his face for a moment. "I was going to stay for only a few days. Until Granddad got back."

"Sheriff Rosa may ask you to stick around a bit longer than that. At least until this situation is resolved."

I laughed. "Why?"

"Let's just say you're an involved party, Rachael." He hesitated, then went on. "The sheriff has requested I make sure you don't get in the way of the investigation, but make sure you stay in town."

"Is that what that conversation was about?"

He had the grace to look embarrassed. "He's got a lot riding on the outcome of this case, Rachael."

I was flabbergasted. "You weren't kidding earlier, about your role in this. Keeping an eye on me."

"No. I wasn't. I'm sorry."

I rapped my fingernails on my brace. "Let me guess. This crime is the perfect showcase for our dear sheriff's crime-solving talents. Election time must be coming."

"First of next month." Nick hesitated before speaking again. "The sheriff is a good man, Rachael. Been doing this for a long time. But he hasn't made it a habit to keep up with things. Relies on old methods and old attitudes. He doesn't cotton much to a highfalutin cop like you being involved."

"And you don't either."

He smiled. "Of course I don't feel that way. But if you don't follow the sheriff's request to keep out of the investigation, I'm supposed to make sure you do."

"I thought you weren't part of the department anymore."

He grinned. "Once a cop, always a cop." He nodded to my leg. "Doubt that stops you, either."

I rolled my eyes in annoyance. "And you think you'll be able to control me?"

"No. Not from what I know about you."

That was a good thing. Because I had no intention of sitting around waiting for the killer to be found. Granddad was going to be devastated. His dream of retirement looked to be over, at least for now.

I felt weary again and leaned my head back against the wall. I closed my eyes. A warm hand touched my shoulder, gave it a gentle squeeze, then released. Opening my eyes, I found myself looking straight up into Nick's eyes, close enough to see they were actually hazel, not brown.

"You need to go home," he said.

"Is that an order?"

"If it needs to be."

I had to laugh. "I'm okay."

He raised an eyebrow in skepticism. "You saw Malik this morning, didn't you?"

"Yes, I did."

"Then you definitely need a good rest."

"How do you know I was at Malik's?"

"You haven't been gone that long. Small town—"

I smirked. "Oh, yeah. Everybody knows everybody's business—before they even do themselves."

"Something like that. Actually, Malik and I are on the same softball team. He told me you were coming." Nick moved past me and glanced out the window. "Things are clearing out now. Not much more to be done here."

I, too, looked out the window. Marshall waved, then headed toward us. I quickly turned to Nick. "Back to this keeping-an-eye-on-me business. Just how do you plan to do that?"

The lopsided grin resurfaced. "Guess I could place you under house arrest. Or. . . ."

"Or?"

He leaned against the wall and crossed his arms, mimicking my earlier pose. "Oh, I suppose I'll just hang around. Make myself a pest."

I laughed. "Like you did when you were a kid?"

"You didn't mind so much then. Admit it."

"Ha. You were insufferable."

"But cute."

I opened my mouth to retort, but he had me there. The door banged open, saving me from a response.

"Rachael?"

I sighed. "In here, Marshall."

My ex walked into the room where Nick and I stood shoulder to shoulder, our backs to the window. Why did I feel like I'd been caught robbing the cookie jar? Marshall looked at me first, then at Nick, with what I swear was hostility.

I frowned. "What's wrong, Marshall?"

His expression was shielded. "You ready to go?"

"Are we through here, Mr. Rittenour?"

Nick smiled briefly at me. "Actually, you do need to come down to the station and make a report. I can take you, if you like."

Marshall interrupted. "What for? She doesn't know anything."

I felt like kicking him. "Thanks a lot."

"I didn't mean it that way, but you know what I mean."

Kicking wasn't good enough. "Look. Why don't you go get Lauren and take her horseback riding?" I glanced at the clock, which hung next to the Glory Wall. "It's only eleven."

Marshall looked like he wanted to argue, but Nick interrupted. "Best get on with normal things, Mr. Grant. For your daughter's sake, I mean. But I'm certain Sheriff Rosa will want you to come by the station later, alone, and give a statement yourself."

"Well, all right," Marshall said. "Rachael, you sure?"

I nodded, fighting my impatience. "What time will you bring Lauren home?"

"About five?"

"Perfect." That would give me most of the afternoon. I had to find out where Granddad was, break the news to him. And find Carmita.

Once Marshall closed the door behind him, I felt a wave of adrenaline surge back. There was a lot to be done. Even the torturous throbbing of my leg felt distant. I turned to my companion. "Okay, Retired Deputy Rittenour. Let's get with keeping me out of trouble."

"Yes, ma'am."

"And, Rittenour?"

"Yes?"

"Please don't call me *ma'am*."

Chapter 4

NICK RITTENOUR and my partner, Dave, could have been soul mates. Nick was a lot cuter, though. And single. I leaned back in the seat and held on for dear life, telling myself to stop speculating about my chauffeur's marital status and concentrate on surviving his driving. Behind us the three dogs braced themselves with each turn but didn't seem unduly concerned by their owner's driving.

I am a lousy passenger. Back home in San Antonio, whenever Dave and I were on the streets, I drove. Believe what you want, but women are better drivers. Especially women cops. I've never had an accident while driving a patrol vehicle, nor while driving the "Cloud," Lauren's not-so-affectionate name for my old white Chevy.

Compare that to Dave's record, which is horrendous. I think he grew up dreaming he'd be another Richard Petty, but he was forced to settle for a revved-up Ford Taurus to make a living. Dave scares me half to death with his driving, and only on rare occasions do I agree to let him have the wheel.

By the time Nick and I arrived at the sheriff's office, I was sweating, swearing, and vowing to get even. We pulled into the parking lot and screeched to a stop. Had it not been for the seat belt, I would have gone right through the windshield and busted up my other leg. Yet I was grateful for the distraction Nick's driving provided; it kept me from thinking about him. We got out of the car, the dogs following.

Nick grinned at my expression as they bolted ahead of him and waited eagerly at the door. "The receptionist has treats for them," he explained.

"Regulars here, huh?"

"Absolutely. Come on." The sheriff's office buzzed with

activity. Several men and one woman in uniform milled about the office, talking about the murder, nodding to me as Nick, his hand resting on my shoulder, steered me toward an empty office. I tried to ignore the raised eyebrows and the winks passed to Nick.

Small towns, small towns. Oh, help me, small towns.

After I gave a brief statement and promised to come back in the next day or two to sign it, we rounded up the dogs and headed back to Nick's vehicle. An unmarked police car drove up at that moment and pulled to a stop.

I peered through the back window and pulled back in surprise. "Hogey?"

The driver of the vehicle stepped out of his car and blocked me. "Excuse me, ma'am."

"That's my cousin in there. Why do you have him?"

The man glanced at Nick, who had walked up behind me. "Rittenour?"

Nick nodded. "Miles. What's going on here?"

Miles's partner, whom I hadn't noticed before, popped open her door and got out. She yanked open the back door and eased Hogey out, none too kindly. His head bobbed toward me, his eyes wide open and scared. His chest rose and fell in short little bursts. He still wore the Grateful Dead T-shirt he'd had on the day before—though I suspected he owned a closet full of them in assorted shades of black.

"Rachael! They think I did it! I didn't do it, I swear!"

"Hogey, calm down. It's all right," I said. I whipped my head around. "Miles, or whatever your name is, why is Hogey under arrest?"

Miles looked right over my head at Nick. "He's not under arrest. We're just bringing him in for questioning."

I nearly thwacked the man with my crutch. Nick eased up behind me and touched my arm. I pulled away, resenting the "calm down" gesture. The dogs, picking up on the excitement, jostled around me, whining for attention.

"Dammit," I said, "*I'm* the one who asked. Answer *me*."

Nick said, "Rachael, it's all right."

"Who is she?" Miles asked Nick, over my head again.

"Rachael!" Hogey wailed.

I clenched my hands so tight around my crutches that my torn palms screamed with the abuse. "Are you going to talk to me or what?"

"Why should I?" Miles snapped. "Who are you?"

I took a deep breath. This was going nowhere. "I'm Hogey's cousin. Rachael Grant. I just want to know why you're doing this. You've scared him half to death."

"Maybe he has a reason to be scared."

I rolled my eyes. "Hogey's drunk half the time, but he wouldn't hurt a cockroach. You guys can't believe he'd kill Stanley."

Miles answered, "I can't say, ma'am. The sheriff just said to bring him in. He's not under arrest."

"Rachael," Nick cut in. "He'll be all right."

"But—"

"They're just asking him a few questions, Rachael. I knew they were going to bring him in."

I wanted to stay angry. They still could have handled Hogey a little more kindly, in my opinion. There was no love lost between my cousin and me, but that didn't matter. He was still family. "If Hogey says they did anything to hurt him in there, Sheriff Rosa will have me to deal with, Nick."

The darn man chuckled. "I think he knows that." He opened the door for me, taking my crutches as I reluctantly eased inside. "Where to next?"

I hesitated, trying to shake off the fear in Hogey's eyes. Why was he so frightened? I'd have to talk to him. Alone.

When Nick got in the car, I said, "You said you knew they were going to question him."

"Yes."

"Why Hogey?" I half turned in the seat, much to the dogs' delight. I automatically reached up and petted one of them. I missed Higgins, I realized.

Nick sighed as he inserted his key into the ignition. It turned and the car roared to life. "What do you know about a money clip he carries?"

"The one my grandfather gave him? What about it?"

"It was found on the premises. It had a lot of money in it."

I turned back in my seat and stared straight ahead. I wasn't going to say another word—not until I talked to Hogey. I saw my plans to return to San Antonio fly away into the sky. There was no way Lauren and I could go home now. Especially if they ended up arresting Hogey. Which, of course, would be ridiculous. "I want to see Stanley."

"Rachael—"

"Now hold on, I just want to see the wounds for myself. Do they do the autopsies here or send them to another county?"

"We have a part-time pathologist. She's a friend of mine. I don't know if she's working today or not."

"Can we find out?"

He sighed. "I suppose if I took you home, you'd turn right around and call the hospital anyway."

"Absolutely."

He put the gear in reverse and backed up. "All right. We'll go see Stanley."

"Do me a favor, though."

"What's that?"

"I'd appreciate it if you'd drive more like Grandma Moses."

His eyes twinkled. "Yes, ma'am. I'll do my best."

Two seconds later we were peeling around the corner toward the hospital. "Not Grandma Moses in the Indy 500, Nick!"

I finally had my breath back by the time we made it to the hospital's back entrance. The dogs stayed outside this time, tied to a bicycle rack.

"You sure they'll be okay?"

"We won't be long."

Nick opened the door for me and then, once we were inside, steered me toward an elevator. I knew which direction it went. Down.

I'd been in the Saddle Gap Memorial Hospital's morgue once before, on a high school class tour. One of those "scared straight" type things, before the program even had a name. I think I was the only one in my class who didn't freak out that afternoon when we met Charlie, a forty-something homeless man who had abused both his body and his mind. He'd been murdered, but he'd withdrawn from life so effectively, he had no one left who cared. But I did. When his murderer was finally caught, I baked a cake in Charlie's honor.

The equipment designed to examine the dead fascinated me. The Presidio County coroner back then had been an ancient gentleman, Dr. Bennett, who took great delight in showing the class his jars of shotgun-laced livers, deformed brains, and his special treasure, a five-chambered heart. The boys all bet it was a calf's heart and made grandiose plans to steal it. All boast, of course, as teenagers then and now are wont to do.

Dr. Bennett also regaled us with his favorite cases in which he helped the local police. I peppered the doctor with questions, and truly believe that day was the first time my interest in criminology was sparked. I always wanted to come back to visit him, but my real life took a different route.

Dr. Bennett was long gone now. Instead, a Mexican American woman, not much older than myself, wearing blue jeans, a red shirt, and a long white lab coat, sat at a table scattered with papers. She held a small tape recorder in her right hand, her thumb on the pause button.

Large, black-rimmed glasses balanced on her nose, and she chewed on the end of a pen as she sifted through the papers. An assortment of similarly abused writing utensils lay scattered about on the desk. Her foot tapped in time to the classical music drifting softly from an unknown source. Five metal tables occupied the room, but only two were accompanied by bags. One, I hoped, held Stanley.

Nick walked up to the woman at the table, waving for me to follow. "Hey, Marisol," he said.

The woman raised her chewed-up pen in greeting. "Hey, Nick. What are you doing here?"

"Came to see Fletcher. This is a friend of mine. Rachael Grant. Rachael, this is Dr. Marisol Flores."

"Nice to meet you," I said.

The woman nodded. "My pleasure. Hope you're not the squeamish type," she said as she picked up a chart.

"I'm not, I promise."

"Rachael's a cop," Nick added. "She'll do fine."

"So why the interest in Stanley?" she asked as she turned off the radio. The sudden lack of music pushed the grimness of the room up a notch.

"Rachael's grandfather owned Tumbleweeds."

"Ah," she said. Pushing a button on her tape recorder, she walked over to one of the tables and pulled back the sheet. *Hello there, Stanley.*

Marisol looked up at Nick and winked. "Case number 02-405. Stanley Eugene Fletcher, approximately 47 years of age. Well-nourished Caucasian male. Gray hair, brown eyes. The body weighs 142 pounds." In a light Spanish accent, she ticked off a litany of facts about Stanley as she waved Nick and me over.

"There is a single entry wound, left anterior chest wall. Entry wound consistent with stabbing utilizing the broad tip of a hunting arrow."

Her voice trailed off and she frowned. She flicked the recorder off. "D'you know that we've always called our folks down here *Stanley? Stanley One, Stanley Two.* Like that. And now we have a real one. Go figure. The women are called *Bertha.* I haven't had enough time to attend to all the particulars yet." She waved to the other table, taking a quick breath. "Been a busy day. Auto accident. Nasty case. I need a couple more hours."

"I know. Just thought we'd drop by and see what you could tell us."

Marisol stood and arched her back. "Well, definitely the first time I've had a case like this."

I motioned toward the wound. "You said he was stabbed?"

She nodded and frowned. "Yes. I think whoever did it wanted it to appear that he was shot with a compound bow. But the arrow, which initially missed the vital organs, was used a second time to stab the subject again. It's a vicious wound, all right, but not vicious enough to kill him alone."

"So, what did?"

Marisol frowned again, then peered at me through her massive lenses. "Not sure. Rittenour, were any drinks, cans, anything, found around the body?"

"Picked up a few."

I interjected, "There was a Coke can still in the office. Half drunk."

"Isn't that just typical," she said in disgust. "Sometimes, the incompetence of these people amazes me. Why wasn't it brought in?"

"I wondered that myself," I said.

She sighed. "Okay. I need to check it as soon as possible. I assume the crime scene is still intact?"

"They let me in there," I pointed out.

"Great. Just great," she muttered. "Nick? Call for me, will you? I might tear the Sheriff's ear off if I talk to him. Of all the stupid oversights."

He nodded. "Can I use your phone?"

"Sure."

As Nick made his phone call, I turned back to look at Stanley. "How long do you think he'd been there?"

"Six to eight hours at the most. I'll know better once I run all the tests. So," she said, her eyes dancing with amused interest. "You working with Rittenour now?"

"No, not exactly. Stanley was buying Tumbleweeds from my grandfather."

"Ouch."

"Yeah, no kidding."

She nodded at my leg. "What happened to you?"

"I'm here on medical leave—came down for some peace and quiet," I said, finding it impossible to keep the irony from my voice.

"Double ouch. Well, somebody sure wanted to ruin your vacation. Or maybe put an end to Stanley's plans to buy the ranch."

I immediately thought of Hogey but dismissed him again. It had to be someone else. "Yeah, but the question is, why?"

"That's what I hope to find out," she said. "Where are you staying?"

"A friend's cabin on the river. It's empty most of the time, and he's letting me and my daughter stay there."

She smiled. "The gay guys' place? I know where that is. Nice."

I would have to talk to Mac. His cover was obviously an

illusion. "Very nice."

"How old is your daughter?"

"Thirteen."

Marisol nodded in understanding. "I have a 14-year-old stepdaughter. She's a handful, but basically a good kid."

Nick hung up the phone and walked back over. "Rosa's sending someone over to Tumbleweeds to get the Coke can. And he's trying to find you, Rachael."

"He doesn't know I'm with you?"

Nick shook his head and grinned. "No. But he wants you to come back in."

"I'd rather go home. I need to make some phone calls. I have to go by the sheriff's office tomorrow anyway, and maybe by then I'll have something more to tell him about Granddad's whereabouts." I yawned, covering my mouth, but not my grin. "Besides, I haven't had my nap yet today."

"You do look tired," Marisol said. She pursed her lips and shook her head. "Get some rest. I don't want to see you in here," she added.

"Gee, thanks."

Nick headed toward the door. "We need to get going, Marisol. Will you let me know when you find something?"

She tapped her mangled pen against her cheek. "Rittenour, you aren't officially part of this investigation, are you?"

"No, ma'am, I'm not."

She frowned. "Then you know I can't give you copies of the reports without Sheriff Rosa's permission."

"I'm not asking for the report, Marisol. I only want to know what killed him."

Her frown deepened. "Where will you be, Nick? Not that I'm going to tell you anything, that is."

He paused, glanced quickly at me for a moment, then spoke. "If I'm not hanging around the office, I'll be at home. Or. . . ." He looked at me again.

"Or," I said, "you can always try Mac's."

We rounded up the dogs and headed back for Nick's car.

"She's nice," I commented.

"Marisol's the one who got me interested in Border Patrol.

Her brothers are both agents."

"Why Border Patrol?"

He grinned as he pulled out of the parking lot. "Saddle Gap was a bit too quiet for my tastes."

"Nothing ever happens here, huh?"

His laughter filled the entire car. "Not until you showed up. You should've come back sooner, Rachael Grant. Maybe then I wouldn't have been inclined to leave."

I didn't want to touch that one. It was past lunchtime, and my stomach was growling. And I was thirsty, which made me think of the Coke can. I wondered what the sheriff's explanation would be for not picking it up. I glanced at Nick, but his eyes were firmly on the road.

He decided to take the scenic route. As is typical of small Texas towns, a magnificent courthouse was at the heart of the downtown area. The pink granite and wood structure, however, played a different role in Saddle Gap. A fire in the late '70s decimated most of the interior of the courthouse, leaving it a Pepto-Bismol pink and ash-colored shell.

Everything inside—the entire county's birth, marriage, and deed records—was destroyed. For two years the courthouse remained in this condition, all county services having been temporarily moved to a building originally meant for the new elementary school.

Finally, funds were raised and Saddle Gap's residents voted to sell the courthouse and build a new complex. The sheriff's office—as well as the downtown fire station, municipal court, and the new license bureau—moved two blocks west to a modern glass and chrome series of buildings.

It took another five years for the courthouse to sell, but finally an enterprising group of vacationing investors stumbled across the building. After wooing several of the wealthier locals into the deal, they bought it.

The idea had been to transform Saddle Gap into a South Texas Santa Fe, turning the former courthouse into the home of two exclusive restaurants and ten or so classy shops featuring what they thought would attract those discriminate Dallasites, Houstonites, and all the other sophisticated -ites in Texas.

They were only somewhat successful. The original group of investors eventually sold out at a loss, once they discovered the blistering summer Chihuahuan Desert heat sent the droves of Texas vacationers not to Saddle Gap, but to, yes, Santa Fe. Several people I know took hits from that incident, including Pamela's father, a physician. He died soon afterward, and several of the other local investors were forced to completely start over.

I was already in San Antonio by the time this happened and didn't get to witness the eventual resurgence of downtown Saddle Gap. The new owners of the courthouse were a lot smarter. They knew what was needed—a place to shop for both locals and visitors, such as the retirees who spent every winter in the Valley and liked to bring back unique gifts to their loved ones.

Now The Courthouse, as it was informally known, buzzed with an authentic Mexican restaurant that did more business in one day than the exclusive restaurants had managed in a month. The classy shops gave way to local artisan showcases: a quilt shop, a woodcraft shop, a clothing store for children, a candlemaker, and a homemade candy store. Jenn's successful pepper and chili supply storefront shop sat on the east side of the square. I'd even steered a former thief from San Antonio this direction, and he'd done quite well with his fruit vendor business.

I smiled despite the dour events of the day. Music wafted on the breeze from a trio of flute-playing musicians entertaining a group of retirees. Giant puffy clouds floated overhead, and the breeze brought the faint lingering scent of early-blooming flowers drifting into the car. I sighed.

"Nice, isn't it?"

I glanced at Nick. "Yes, it is."

"Missed it?"

I looked away, wondering how best to answer. "Sometimes," I said.

We pulled to a stop at a light as one of the store owners exited her shop. A rotund, cherubic-faced granny-type dressed in a calico smock, she reminded me of my own grandmother. Her clothes were smudged with bright colors.

She waved cheerfully toward us, and Nick responded with a wave of his own.

"Who was that?"

"You don't recognize Mrs. Bushnell?"

We turned the corner, but I looked back over my shoulder, squinting in disbelief. "High school art teacher?"

"She retired, opened up a craft store, and teaches painting."

"That's nice."

"She's still just as strict."

I laughed. "You take classes from her?"

"Yes, ma'am. I'm good, too."

I raised an eyebrow. "Bet you are."

"Seriously. I'll show you my work. If you'd like. How about dinner tonight?"

Nick drove the car past a number of fruit stands. I searched the crowd for my friend Gilbert, the former thief. He was nowhere in sight. I frowned. For a moment, I thought I saw Jamie talking to a bearded man in filthy khakis, but she walked off before I could be sure. Her companion walked quickly in the other direction. I shrugged.

"Ma'am?"

"Nick, please stop calling me that."

"I will if you'll answer my question. Dinner?"

He turned toward the highway. All I could think about was taking a more or less bath, folding myself into some sweats, and having a sandwich while enjoying the peace and quiet. And maybe I'd even substitute a beer for a Vicodan. I grimaced. No Vicodan. A beer would have to suffice. Or two, or three.

"Rachael?"

"Sorry. My mind was drifting."

"I can fry some fresh catfish. And some fries, and I've got one of Carmita's apple pies."

"All right, all right, I give in! But can we wait till Thursday?"

"Sure."

"Great. I'm looking forward to it."

Nick threw the car's engine into high gear, slamming me back into the seat.

"However," I added. "I think I'll take a cab."

Chapter 5

NICK AND I PASSED OUT OF DOWNTOWN and headed toward the river. We approached the grocery store of grocery stores— once one of the main hangouts for high school groupies— the Saddle Gap Piggly Wiggly Number Two. The original Piggy Wiggly's roof collapsed not once, but twice, in freak rain- storms, and the owners, convinced the property was jinxed, rebuilt on a different site. Fortunately for the Gap, the new store was built in record time; the only other supermarket around was thirty minutes away, though the local Smarties did a brisk business every night after twelve.

"Nick, could you do me a favor?"

"Sure."

"I'd really appreciate it if you would drop me off at the store. I can take a cab home. I don't have a thing to eat back at the cabin."

"Sure. I can wait out here for you, though. No reason to take a cab."

"You don't mind?"

He shook his head as he pulled into a parking space. "I can run in for you if you like."

"No, I'll do it. I'm not sure what I want."

"Take your time." He pulled a book from beneath his seat and held it up so I could see the title. *Rage Sleep.* "I'm always prepared."

"I've read that. Good book."

Nick simply nodded as he opened the book at his marker, a neatly folded gum wrapper.

I pushed the door open and got out, pulling my crutches after me. Bending down, I looked through the open window. The boxer stuck her head out and I patted it. "Thanks, Nick. I'll be right back."

He grunted a reply, not looking up.

One of the hardest things I'd had to deal with, growing up as a teenager in Saddle Gap, was the small-town penchant for making big news out of the littlest of things. Even going to the grocery store accompanied by a good-looking man like Nick would immediately set off the gossip chain; we'd be married in a week, with me expecting twins. So I was glad he opted to stay in the car and wait, though perhaps even that action would be noted.

I wondered about his reasons for leaving Saddle Gap, and if part of it wasn't similar to the reasons why I had left.

I grabbed a cart and put one of my crutches inside, using the cart and the other crutch for balance. Already, from where I stood at the head of the bread aisle, I could see two girls who had gone to high school with me. But it wasn't the first one, Staci Helbring, who captured my attention. It was the second.

I'd recognize that flame-red hair and those swinging hips anywhere; even fourteen years later, Pamela Pianka still dressed like a whore.

I picked up a loaf of bread, threw it in the basket, and moved down the aisle, doing my best to ignore her. I passed two friends of my grandmother's and nodded to them. One of the stockers waved to me. What was his name? Charles? Chuckie? That was it. Chuckie Martin. I waved back, but I couldn't shift my awareness off *her*.

Jamie was right—Pamela was here, in Saddle Gap. But why? Her parents were long gone. There was no reason for her to be here.

I turned the corner and there she was. For a long moment we stood, face to face, not ten feet apart. For once in my life I didn't know what to do. Despite her outrageous outfit— low-cut peasant top and a too short skirt, with heels, of course—she wore only a little makeup, which failed to cover the fatigue around her eyes.

A brief glimpse of the girl who had once been my friend flashed before me. I looked away. I decided, despite the fact I'd hosted a thousand different scenarios in my mind—all equally vicious, to exact my revenge on Pamela Pianka—

when it came time to do it, I couldn't. I started to turn away, when she spoke.

"Rachael, wait."

I stopped. "Why?"

She shot a glare toward those watching. They scattered. She walked up to me, her expression guarded. "I was hoping to run into you."

"What do you want, Pamela?" All right, so I was still feeling a little defensive—even after all these years.

"Don't you think it's about time we let bygones be bygones, Rachael?"

"Isn't it a little late to make amends?"

A pained look crossed her face. "Please, Rachael. You don't know what it's like, living here, being blamed for something I didn't do."

"Something you didn't do? Excuse me, Pamela. I don't feel like talking to you right now. I've got more important things on my mind."

"Everyone adores you, Rachael. Everything was fine until you came back. Why did you have to? You're ruining everything."

"I don't know what you're talking about." I tried to take off, but she stopped me.

"Wait."

"Let go of my cart. You've already got what you wanted of mine. Can't you be satisfied with that?"

The look of perplexed horror on her face surprised me. "You know?"

Now I was the one confused. "What are you talking about?"

"Nothing. I'm sorry." She backed away. One step, two. Then she turned and hurried off. I watched after her, baffled by her strange behavior. I even thought about going after her, but the day had taken its toll on me.

After throwing a bunch of frozen dinners on top of the bread, I headed for the checkout. I know the checkout lady asked me a few questions about how I was enjoying being back, which I must have answered, but my thoughts were on Pamela. I tried to put the encounter out of my mind, but it simply stood out beside everything else bizarre that had gone on since arriving the day before.

I knew I should have stayed in San Antonio.

At Mac's at last, I watched from the safety of my doorway as Nick drove off. Once his vehicle had turned the corner, I breathed a sigh of relief, though I'd be hard-pressed to say whether it was because I was no longer at the mercy of his driving, or no longer at the mercy of those eyes. I was glad he was willing to wait for a delay to the dinner, and to agree to my insistence on being delivered by cab. I wasn't ready to subject myself to either him or his driving again until I sorted out my feelings.

For now, though, I had more important things to worry about. After locking the door, I eased gratefully into the living area. Sitting in the middle of the room, as nonchalantly as you please, was the wayward brown suitcase. *Hallelujah! Vicodan!*

Lauren and her father must have run past the cabin on their way to horseback riding and found the suitcase on the front porch, then brought it inside.

I hobbled over, picked it up, and opened the latches. A quick search revealed everything had arrived safely except for one thing. My medicine. Great.

I threw a Stouffer's macaroni and cheese (the ultimate comfort food) into the microwave, grabbed a couple of cans of Vernors from the fridge, and headed toward the bathroom. Halfway there I set the cans on the floor and, with my crutch, rolled them in the general direction of the couch.

After taking a quick sponge bath, I pulled on my rather tattered but favorite flannel gown and hauled a quilt from my hosts' bed toward the living room. A glance assured me the mac and cheese still had a few minutes to go.

I herded the Vernors cans closer to the couch and curled up as best I could with the telephone and a pen and paper. I had some phone calls to make before Lauren got home, and as it was already 4:30, I hadn't much time.

From where I sat, I could see through the back windows to the lawn. A circular trampoline perched at a slightly awkward angle, leaning toward a small boat ramp.

A red-and-silver fishing boat floated on the water, its single gray-haired occupant, pole in hand, so still the whole scene almost looked like a painting. I knew I'd have to try to go fishing at least once while I was here.

First, though, other things commanded my attention. Vicodan. A quick phone call to my doctor's office in San Antonio was all that was needed to have the prescription filled locally. Now I just had to wait to hear from the pharmacy that it was in. Hopefully it wouldn't take too long.

Then I tried to call Carmita at Tumbleweeds. No answer, and I didn't want to leave a voice mail, so I hung up.

No one answered at Granddad's house, either. After the torture session with Malik the next morning, I'd have to convince Jamie to run me by the house to take a closer look and see if I could ferret out any hints to where Granddad had gone.

I also wanted to run by Tumbleweeds. I wanted to look for a phone list of the employees so I could contact them. Maybe one of them knew where Carmita could have gone. And I had to talk to Hogey as soon as possible. He didn't have a telephone, though, so I'd have to wait.

Next, I called Jenn at her store. I started grinning the moment I heard her voice. "Hot Mamma Salsa and Chili Supply," she said in a well-practiced rush. "How'd you like to come try our special of the day? Rocking Rocotillo Salsa, its fiery ingredients fresh from Mexico. One quart of Mamma's finest for under five bucks. Guaranteed to make even the laziest caballero move to the beat."

"More like move to the nearest bottle of Maalox."

"Rachael!" I had to hold the phone away from my ear as her laughter boomed through the phone. "Where the heck are you? I haven't heard from you in weeks, kiddo. What's going on?"

"Jenn, calm down. I'm in town."

"Woman, why didn't you tell anyone you were coming? Afraid the bandwagon would be rolled out?"

I sighed. "A lot of good it did. I feel like I've been here a month already, I've been so inundated."

"You have plans tonight?"

I smiled. "I was hoping you'd come by tomorrow. Would that be okay?"

"Absolutely. I've got tons to tell you. Where are you staying? At Mac's? Did you bring Lauren? Higgins? How long will you be here?"

"Slow down. We'll be here for about a week; and yes, we're at Mac's; and no, I didn't bring the dog."

"Rachael, guess who moved back to Saddle Gap."

"I know. I ran into her at the grocery store."

"Dang. Wish I'd been there. What else has been going on? We've had a quiet day, so I've been in the back sorting through all the stuff I brought back from Mexico, but someone said something about Stanley Fletcher going to buy Tumbleweeds, and then getting killed? Is that true?"

"Unfortunately. I'll tell you all about it when you come. Oh! And, Jenn?" I paused. *Should I say something?* "Nothing. Never mind."

"All right, Rachael. What's up? Come on, tell me."

"Have you seen Nick today?"

"I have a message from him, in fact. He wants me to make some of my Mariachi Mango and Lime Salsa for Thursday night. Goes great with fish. Did I tell you he's going into the Border Patrol?"

Great with fish. Hmm. "No, you didn't."

"My parents had a fit. I told Dad that Nicky was old enough to take care of himself. But he *is* the baby." She chuckled. "Hard to believe the pest has grown up."

"Yes."

She cleared her throat. "Rachael, why'd you ask about Nick?"

"No reason. See you tomorrow, Jenn."

"Rachael Grant, don't you dare do this to me!"

"Bye, sweetheart, see you later!"

"Wench."

I chuckled as I hung up, feeling much better. I still had one more phone call to make.

As I listened to the phone ringing, I leaned my head back and stared through the window, across the river. The microwave beeped, cheerfully announcing that my lunch/dinner was ready. I had no choice but to ignore it, as my partner finally made it on the line and said hello.

"Dave!"

"Rachael, what are you calling here for?"

I grumbled. "Thanks a lot. How is she doing?" The microwave beeped again.

"Who?"

I could almost see him, rolling his eyes innocently toward the ceiling, rocking back and forth on his heels.

"Margaret, you brat." The microwave beeped once more.

"Ah, your replacement? Maggie's doing fine. Just fine."

The microwave beeped, this time more impatiently. "Traitor," I told him.

"Hey, man, she lets me do the driving. What's up, Rachael? And what's that beeping?"

"Just dinner. Dave, I need some help."

"Help? Why?"

I took a deep breath. "Hold on." I placed the phone on the pillow and clumsily hopped toward the microwave. The action made my leg sing. I'd already put it through more torture in one day than I had the past two weeks, and I had a feeling the night was going to be even worse. No Vicodan, I reminded myself. Lovely.

Pulling out a plate from the cabinet, I slid the hot dish onto it. A bottle of Extra Strength Tylenol sat on the counter, beckoning me. A quick flick of the wrist, and it sailed through the air, landing with a satisfying *plunk* on the phone's receiver. A muffled "Hey!" was my reward.

"Sorry!" I yelled. I looked longingly back at the refrigerator and the two beers tucked inside, finally grabbing one. I just hoped a Tylenol-and-beer cocktail wouldn't land me on one of good Dr. Flores's slabs. Moving slower than a slug, I finally collapsed onto the couch, mac and cheese in hand.

"Rachael?"

"Here, here. Hold on, Dave." I balanced the phone with my shoulder and, with my bad leg propped up on the couch, proceeded to stir my cheese and continue on. "Where's Fernando, Dave."

Silence. When Dave finally answered, his voice had slowed to a country-boy drawl. "Well, Rachael, we don't exactly know."

I tensed and stopped my fork in mid-stir. "You don't exactly know? What is that supposed to mean?"

"Rachael, I was actually going to call you tonight. He's picked up his little campaign."

"What has he done?"

"Been sending letters to the station, phoning in threats, slopping graffiti everywhere, stuff like that. Juvenile, but we're taking it seriously."

"Graffiti? Where?"

Silence. Then, "On the side of your condo. Some pretty nasty stuff. I already had it painted over," he added hurriedly.

"Damn him," I hissed, closing my eyes. Dave was only telling me half of Fernando's message, I knew. "Thanks, Dave. But do me a favor and go by my place tomorrow, okay? My next-door neighbor is getting my mail. Fernando might have sent stuff there."

"Mrs. Kravitz? She hates me," he said in mock horror.

I smiled, appreciating my partner's attempt at cheering me up. "That's just because you mowed down her roses with your car. I'll call her and let her know, okay? Send it to me overnight."

"All right, all right. I can still make the last pickup if I hurry."

"Thanks." I heard a car pull to a stop outside the house. "Got to go. Lauren's here."

"What else is going on, Rachael?"

The car door slammed.

"There's been a murder, Dave. All I have is a name, Stanley Fletcher. I'll try to get more information on him tomorrow and call you back."

"Something actually happened down there?"

"Yeah. I'll tell you about it tomorrow."

A deep sigh came through the phone. When he spoke, Dave's voice was full of concern. "Rachael, I'm sure Fernando's still around here."

"I don't think this was his handiwork, either, but I'd still feel better if he was locked up."

"I know, partner. Me too."

The front door started to rattle, and a muffled "Mom" drifted through.

"Talk to you tomorrow, Dave. Okay?"

"Okay. And be careful down there."

"Thanks. And be nice to Margaret, you hear? Tell her I said she can drive, too."

A chuckle was Dave's reply.

I'd just hung up the phone when Lauren burst in through the door, her father right behind her. Great. And here I sat in just my ragged nightgown, stuffing my face with mac and cheese. I felt my cheeks heat, but that was all forgotten when Lauren walked over to the brown suitcase and popped it open.

"Hey, cool! Now I can wear these tomorrow," she said, yanking out the missing jeans as she turned to me. "Where'd you find the suitcase?"

"You didn't bring it inside?" I said.

"Nope. Not me."

Marshall raised his hand. "Not me, either."

For once, I believed him. But, if they hadn't brought it inside, who had?

Chapter 6

MY GAZE LOCKED with Marshall's. I shook my head once and was gratified to see he understood. He took a step forward and kissed Lauren on the head. "I'll see you tomorrow, pumpkin. I need to talk to your mom a minute."

"Okay. I'm going to go wash my hair. It's a mess." Lauren hugged her dad, then plunked a kiss on my cheek.

I hated to see the flash of excitement zipping across her face as she headed for her room; but, still a little shook up from the realization someone unknown had entered the river house, I kept my mouth shut.

"Bye, Dad!" she called from the hallway.

"Bye, hon. See you tomorrow."

"Okay. Love you. I love you, too, Mommy."

Mommy? She hadn't called me that in years, but this was the second time in as many days. I turned to Marshall as soon as I was sure Lauren's door had closed. "Would you do me a favor and check all the windows before you go? Please?"

He frowned. "Sure, but what's going on here?"

I shook my head. "Nothing for you to worry about."

"Bullcorn. I saw your face when Lauren dragged out that suitcase."

I fought for patience. Marshall fancies himself hero material, but if it ever came right down to it, I don't think all his bravado would be of much help. Still, I couldn't see a way out of it. "It's nothing, Marshall. I just thought Lauren had brought in the suitcase."

"She said one was missing. Maybe the airport folks sent it over."

"I'd assumed you guys brought it in."

"Nope, not us."

Then how would it have gotten inside? "It's too late to check with the airport tonight, though. I'll call them tomorrow. Still, would you mind checking all the windows for me?" I showed him the palms of my hands, correctly guessing he'd freak when he saw how torn up they were.

"Geez, Rachael. That's from your crutches?"

"Yeah. Hurts worse than my leg."

"Look. There's some stuff the farmers around here use, toughens up the skin. I'll drop a tube by for you tomorrow. Let me see it a second."

"It's all right. I've just been on my crutches too much."

He walked over to me and picked up my hands, shaking his head in disgust. We both stared at my blistered and torn palms for a moment.

Uncomfortable with his scrutiny, I yanked my hands away and hid them beneath my blanket. "Just check the windows. And the back door, too, okay?" I had my gun, of course, but precaution was preferred.

He frowned but then nodded. He knew it wasn't really like me to act so paranoid. "Okay. Sure," he said. He left the room, and I was alone.

I had a sudden, crazy need to hear another voice. I knew I should call the sheriff about the suitcase, but the first number I flipped to in the Saddle Gap phone directory was Nick Rittenour's. I punched in the number before I could stop myself.

"Rittenour."

I paused, glancing toward Lauren's room. "Nick, it's Rachael."

"Rachael. What's wrong?"

I quickly told him about the suitcase's reappearance inside the locked-up house.

"You want me to come by?"

Well, I did—but didn't think it was a good idea. "That's okay," I replied. "Marshall's here."

Silence. "Robbie's on patrol tonight. I'll ask him to drive by, okay?"

"Thanks." I paused again, listening to his breathing, wishing he'd ignore me and head over himself. "I hate this," I said, more to myself than anything.

"Me too," he answered, his voice softly hoarse. "See you Thursday. Dinner at six?"

"Yes. Dinner. Have you heard from the coroner's office yet?"

"Nope. Not yet."

"Darn." I chewed on my thumbnail and stared out the darkened window. I could see the trampoline silhouetted against the river. The fishing boat was gone, but I wondered if the fisherman had seen something. Or maybe the neighbors had. I added checking both to my growing list of things to do.

"I hate this," I repeated. "What about Hogey? Did you hear anything about him?"

"I talked to Miles. They questioned Hogey, but he said he'd dropped the money clip and didn't know where. It had a lot of money in it."

"That doesn't sound like Hogey."

"Didn't think so either. I'm free tomorrow. Do you need a ride to Malik's?"

I grinned. "That's right. You're supposed to keep an eye on me. Fortunately Jamie's picking me up in the morning."

Marshall entered the room. I straightened up on the couch, pulling the blanket tighter over me. "But I'll be free later to come to the station, Deputy."

"The ex just walked in?"

"Yes, sir."

A chuckle. Then, "Hey, if you get to call me *sir*, I get to call you *ma'am*."

I laughed. "Yes, sir, I guess you're right about that."

"How about I pick you up at Malik's?"

"Only if you promise not to drive like a madman."

Nick chuckled. "I'll try, at least."

I watched as Marshall walked over to the bookshelves. He pulled one of the books out, flipped through it, and then, obviously bored, put it back. I rolled my eyes. He walked over to a window and tugged on it. Locked.

"Ten okay?" Nick asked.

"Ten o'clock should be about right."

I could hear papers rustling over the phone, and he said, "What about Lauren?"

"She'll be with her father."

Silence. "I'll be there at 9:50. Is that acceptable?"

"Yes, sir. Thanks."

Marshall scrutinized me.

"Oh," Nick said, "and how about if I do the same Thursday morning?"

I glanced at Marshall. "Sure. Oh, will I need to bring anything? Anything special?"

"Bring a swimsuit. I have a pool and a hot tub." My alarm must have betrayed me, as he added, "Don't worry, we won't be alone. Malik and his wife have invited themselves over."

"Great. I can't wait. Bye," I said and hung up.

"And?" Marshall said.

"And what? Did you check everything?"

"Who was that?"

I frowned. "A patrol is coming to check on things."

"Why?"

I shrugged. "With what happened to Stanley, I just feel better having someone keep an eye on the place. If you're done checking, you can go on."

He didn't seem to like the idea much. "Rachael, I think I should stay. At least until the patrol comes."

"No, you shouldn't," I said. "I want to take a nap."

"Maybe I should take Lauren with me."

I shook my head. "It would upset her to see us worried. She's probably still in the shower, anyway." A car drove up outside the house. That was fast. Thank heavens. "I bet that's the patrol now."

I stood, wrapped the blanket around me, and hopped to the window. Marshall joined me, peering suspiciously outside. A Presidio County Sheriff's car sat out front.

Marshall frowned but put his hand on the door. "Well, if you need me, call. I'll come right over."

"Okay, I promise. Thanks, Marshall." He closed the door behind him.

I threw the deadbolt into place and examined it, twisting the knob back and forth. No problems, smooth action. I had no way of knowing how many people owned a key, and both the deadbolt and the door lock used the same one. Not smart, really. The windows had only standard locks on them as well.

In this remote area, I was surprised Mac hadn't installed a more sophisticated system. But then, the man lived in a state of illusion—no doubt he thought he and his lover were cocooned, insulated from all the bad guys back home. Saddle Gap was supposed to be a safe haven for them—as I'd thought it would be for Lauren and me.

Maybe I was as naive as Mac.

I heard Marshall start his Jeep. I watched as he rolled to the end of the driveway, pausing for a moment to talk to the deputy in the patrol car. Marshall moved on, but the patrol car stayed put. I assumed Nick had asked the cop to do more than just drive by occasionally. I closed the curtains and tested the front door once more. Locked.

Fighting the urge to double-check the windows after Marshall, I went into the kitchen, dumping my half-eaten mac and cheese into the trash. My appetite had taken a nose-dive. It suited me fine, actually. I patted my tummy and stuck my tongue out at it. The weeks of inactivity were taking their toll. I wasn't much in the way of a bathing beauty right now.

I leaned on the kitchen sink, staring at my reflection in the window. Stick-straight, dark brown hair, with a hint of gray at the temples, hung loosely to the middle of my back. I held my hair up, trying to imagine how I'd look in a chic new haircut. Maybe Jamie was right. I should get it whacked off.

I let the strands slip through my fingers and, sighing in exasperation, grabbed a ponytail holder and pulled my hair back off my face.

Boring brown eyes stared back at me. A light smattering of freckles dotted my nose. I even had a small mole on my cheek. Freckled and scarred on the outside, and not a little scarred on the inside as well.

I couldn't figure what anyone could see in that—especially a younger man like Nick Rittenour. When I was 25, I *knew* anyone over 30 was old. And anyway, I argued with myself, I had no business going out on a date with anyone from Saddle Gap, even a harmless double date. He was leaving here, anyway. He'd said so himself; in one week he'd be off to the Border Patrol Academy. I was leaving in a few days myself, and it would be a long, long time before I came back to Saddle Gap.

This was ridiculous. I had to call Nick and break the date. I went to my room, collapsed on my bed, and turned off the light. It would be easier in the dark. I sat for a long moment, unable to will myself to pick up the phone, realizing with a little bit of shock that I had the man's number memorized.

The phone rang. My heart lurched. Maybe Nick was calling *me*; now reason had set in with him, too.

I sure hoped not.

"Hello?"

Granddad's voice resonated merrily across the miles. "Rachael, honey. How you doing?"

"Granddad!" I bolted upright, fumbling for the light. I nearly knocked the lamp to the floor in my relief to hear from him at last. "Where are you? Where is Carmita?"

"Well, honey, that's why I'm calling. She's with me."

"With you? Thank God." I closed my eyes and sank back into the pillows. My eyes shot open. "Granddad, why didn't you tell me she was going with you?"

"Well, plans just kinda ended up that way."

"That was nice of you to do that for her." I scooted myself upright. "When did she leave here?"

"Well, I picked her up at the airport this afternoon. Why?"

"Is she there now?"

"Nope. She's down getting coffee. Rachael, honey, I know this must come as a shock, but—"

"Granddad, listen to me. Somebody killed Stanley."

"I know, honey. Carmita told me."

I was struck dumb. "She told you? How'd she know?"

"Heard it on the news, coming from El Paso."

My mouth opened like a guppy. "El Paso?"

He chuckled. "Well, she went there to tell her kin, and, well, it all happened kinda quick. I'm still in fine shape, you know, and Carmita's only fifteen years younger'n me, and it just didn't seem right—"

"Tell her kin—" I echoed.

"Her sons. Rachael, honey. Carmita and I got married tonight. On the slopes. I'm sorry, honey. Thought we'd tell you when we got back, but I kinda felt guilty."

Married. And she had sons?

"Rachael?"

Carmita and Granddad? *Granddad and Carmita?*

"You okay, sweetheart?"

I shifted in the blankets, lay slowly back against the pillows, and sighed in relief. "Yes, of course I am. She went to El Paso first?"

"Dropped me off at the airport at three—"

"In the morning?"

"Yup. Early flight's cheaper. Then she drove on up to El Paso, flew right on up here, and off we went. Rachael, I wish you'n Lauren could've been here! We got married up in the mountains, up real high. Snowin', and everyone on skis. We said 'I do' and took off down the slopes, folks behind us carrying torches, acting like crazy fools." He chuckled. "It was quite a sight, Rachael. All them skiers tearing down the mountain, shakin' cans in one hand, whippin' them torches about in the other."

I smiled, envisioning the sight. "It sounds beautiful, Granddad."

"You really okay with it? I know Carmita don't say much, but I'm kinda used to her being around."

"It's fine. Of course. Tell Carmita I said so. I'm going to have to tell the police, though, Granddad."

"Oh. Oh, dear, do they think—"

"I suspect they think Carmita disappeared because. . . ." I didn't want to go there. Carmita a suspect? It was as laughable a thought as Hogey a suspect. "Because they were worried about her." I winced, but he didn't notice.

"She worried about that, too, but I told her that was nonsense. I finalized everything before I left, Rachael."

I was glad to hear that. "I want to talk to her, Granddad. Maybe she heard something, though, or saw something before she left. Ask her to call me tomorrow, okay? After lunch."

"Will you talk to the sheriff? Let him know Carmita's with me?"

"Of course I will. But I think you'd better call him yourself."

"Okay, sweetheart. But don't worry none. I guess I'll have to find out what's gonna happen to Tumbleweeds, though."

"I don't know, Granddad. I'll find out who his next of kin are. We'll worry about that later, though, okay?"

"I left a list of all the employees at the house. You might give 'em a call, let 'em know I'll do what I can when I get back." He paused then said, "Dang it, Rachael. I really don't want to go back to work, but tell them I will, not to worry."

I hated the sadness in his voice. "All right. But let's worry about that when you get back, okay? Have some fun. I'll get Hogey and Cathy to help me keep an eye on things." Hogey. No need to worry Granddad about that now, I thought.

"Sounds good. Okay then."

After a few more minutes, we hung up. I sat for a time, staring at the wall, thinking about Stanley's murder. I couldn't shake the thought that Carmita may not be safe. She might know something or, perhaps, not even realize she did. Maybe she'd overheard something.

Or, looking at the other side of things for a moment, maybe she *was* responsible, and she's just using Granddad as a cover. That woman is always shrouded in mystery, says little. And why didn't I know she had sons? How many? From what Granddad had told me long ago, she'd written off all her people from her life forever. I shook my head in dismay, knowing Carmita wasn't out of the woods yet. Married to Granddad, yeah, but not free and clear.

But then, I supposed, neither was I.

Chapter 7

MY EYES FLEW OPEN, and I twisted my head to the side. The clock on the bedside table blinked just after 5:00 A.M. Not good.

Sleep had evaded me most of the night, and I figured I'd caught two, three hours, at the most. White-hot prickles shot through my leg, my shoulders felt like two twenty-pound cats had slept on them all night, and the mattress was lumpy. Somehow, I had rolled over onto my stomach, my leg cocked awkwardly to the side, my chest squashed. I had no idea how I was going to flip back over again without killing myself.

It was going to be a long day.

I lay for a moment, trying to gather energy to give it a shot, and thought about Granddad. Married, after twelve years of being alone. Wow. I'd been alone even longer, but marriage was not on my mind.

I had to admit that sex sure was, though. That had to be why I reacted so hungrily to Nick. Nothing more than a base reaction. Hormones. I could blame it on hormones.

I squeezed my eyes shut, trying to conjure up the image of someone, anyone, besides Nick Rittenour.

Useless.

Try as I might, I couldn't even remember what my last bed partner looked like, it had been so long ago. I was starving, I realized. Not for food, but for a little cuddling. That's all I needed, then I'd be fine. No ties, no worries about tomorrow, just pure release.

Once I became a cop, most of the love interests I'd had drifted away, intimidated by my Glock, I suppose. Cops are a scary breed. And I had no wish to date any of my fellow officers. I was too busy being a mom, anyway, trying to get Lauren grown and independent.

I'd always told myself, "when Lauren's a teenager" I would expend the effort to hook up with someone. I really didn't want to spend my entire life alone, after all. But that time had always seemed so far away, nothing to worry about. Easy to ignore.

Lauren turned 13 five months ago, and I'd found other excuses to remain unattached. Relationships are scary. I'd been burned once before, and it was far easier to stay single.

Easier, but darn lonely.

Granddad had discovered that and, apparently, found love only a foot away. I had to smile. It was kind of neat, but I would feel better once I was entirely sure Carmita was in the clear. Then I would celebrate for him in grand style.

I wondered what Granddad would do about Tumbleweeds now. Had the killer thought the transaction was incomplete? Did the potential sale of the ranch have anything to do with Stanley's death at all? Maybe there was a glitch. Maybe Tumbleweeds was still Granddad's.

Maybe I needed to figure out why that thought made me smile.

I glared at the clock. Ten minutes past five. Giving up, I slid out of bed, grimacing at the pain as I tried to stand. I leaned on the post, fighting for breath as bullets of pain ripped not just through my knee, but through my shoulders and my hands as well. And my armpits. Man, they hurt. Darn crutches.

Exhaustion pulled at me. I had no idea how I would make it through the day.

By half past five I managed to get some coffee going. As I waited for it to finish brewing, I stared out the windows toward the river.

No little boats, not at this time of the morning. In another thirty minutes or so, the river would be dotted with early-morning fishermen, trying to catch the evening's meal. But now the river slid past, dark and silent, an occasional leaping fish the only disturbance to its surface.

I took a deep breath and smiled. Fresh-brewed coffee. I poured a cup into a thermos bottle, threw in a Sweet 'n Low and some milk, capped it, and half-hopped over to the couch. The thermos had been Lauren's idea. Smarty Pants came up with it *after* I'd burned myself while trying to navigate with a full cup.

I hadn't folded the blanket from the night before, so I threw it over myself. The room was a little nippy. Once settled in, I took a sip of coffee, set the thermos aside, and closed my eyes.

Someone banged on the front door. I sat up with a start, blinking rapidly in confusion.

"Rachael? You in there?"

Jamie? I glanced at the kitchen clock. 6:50. I'd nodded off. "Hold on," I called out, making my way toward the door. I quickly unlocked it, and she barreled in, two huge grocery bags balanced precariously in her arms.

"Thought you might be hungry. Got some more Vernors, too."

I laughed, incredulous, as I followed her into the kitchen. "You didn't have to do that, Jamie."

"I was at the store for Mom, so I thought, what the heck?" She plunked the grocery bags down on the counter and proceeded to dig through them. "Marshall told me about yesterday. That's really awful about Stanley."

I grimaced. "Yeah. No kidding. Did you know him?"

She shrugged as she pulled out the six-pack. "No, not really, though he's been around a while. Ran an insurance agency, I think. He was the only one of the courthouse guys who didn't leave."

"I didn't realize that he was involved."

"Uh-huh. The others hightailed it. He was kinda weird. Those goofy outfits really made him look ridiculous." She rolled her eyes and pulled out a small white sack and tossed it to me.

I peered inside and breathed in. Cinnamon. Pecans. Yum-yum. "I'll never get back into my uniform if I eat one of these."

She laughed and yanked some apples out of the sack. "That's okay. I don't want you to go back to San Antonio, anyway."

"Trying to fatten me up on purpose, then?"

She nodded solemnly. "Whatever it takes."

I considered the cinnamon rolls. "Well, maybe one wouldn't hurt."

"Good girl," Jamie said. "Those aren't quite Carmita's cinnamon rolls, but they'll do in a pinch." With her foot, she pulled out the refrigerator's fruit drawer and began placing the apples in, one by one. "The apples will balance your sinful indulgence."

I paused in mid-bite. "Jamie, did you know Carmita and my granddad were seeing each other?"

The rest of the apples tumbled into the drawer, and she whirled around. "Your grandfather and Carmita? Really?"

"I talked to him last night. Carmita was with him."

Jamie yanked the sack off the counter and turned back to the refrigerator, throwing the rest of the food inside. "No. I didn't know. He never said anything to me. Neither did she. Not a word." She whirled around to me again. "Are you sure? No one ever tells me anything, anymore. I'm stuck in Mom's house most of the time, you know." Her face crumpled, and I reached out to her, alarmed.

"Jamie, are you okay?"

She nodded, then shook her head, rubbing her face with her hands. "I'm sorry. I . . . I didn't get much sleep last night."

"Emma?"

She lifted her head, nodding. "Yeah. Mom's in such pain, Rachael. And I can't seem to do anything to help her." Her face crumpled again. "Oh, Rachael, sometimes I just get so tired. . . ."

As I had when she was a little girl, I found myself cradling Jamie in my arms. She had been close to Lauren's age now when Marshall and I started dating, and she had often tagged along after us. She'd been a cute kid. We'd developed a big sister/little sister relationship that eventually had turned into friendship.

Sometimes, though, that wasn't enough. I hugged her, then held her away from me, searching her face. "You're exhausted," I said. "I shouldn't have asked you to cart me around, on top of everything else."

Jamie wiped her tears as she fought to regain her composure. "No, it's okay. I've missed you."

I smiled. "Missed you too, kiddo." I'd definitely have to talk to Marshall about Jamie. "Maybe I can give you a break taking care of Emma."

"No, that won't be necessary." She smiled. "We get on okay. Marshall helps me do things when he's not at work. I just didn't get enough sleep last night."

"You sure? I could read to her or something."

"Don't worry about it. Honest. Besides, you look like you're hurting, yourself."

I groaned, stretching my aching back, and wincing. "My leg, my back, my butt." I held out my hands. "Everything hurts."

"Yuck! You know, Marshall has some stuff that might help that."

"I know. He's going to bring some by later—some horse-hoof slop or something."

She grinned. "Actually, it's for cow teats. It really works, though." Her gaze darted over my shoulder. "Hi, Lauren."

"Good morning," Lauren said, her words garbled by a yawn. She wore a Chicago Cubs T-shirt, courtesy of my partner, who was originally from Illinois. She cradled her much-worn Tom Kitten in one arm.

She'd had that thing since she was a baby, and still slept with it. Except at sleepovers, of course. I figured it would be the first thing we packed when she went off to college.

"What time is it?" Lauren asked, brushing her bangs out of her eyes.

"Seven-fifteen."

"I thought I heard something crash or something."

Jamie smiled. "Sorry. I dropped the apples."

"S'okay. Mom, can I sleep over at Skipper's?"

"I don't know, honey. Who is Skipper? A girl or boy?" These days, with her friends' names, it was often hard to tell.

"Girl, Mom. She said her mom already met you."

"Who?"

"I think she works at the hospital or somewhere."

I frowned. "What's her name?"

"Don't know."

"What's Skipper's last name?"

"Don't know."

I looked at Jamie in exasperation, and she shrugged. Lauren was oblivious.

I'd met only one person at the hospital, and that was Marisol Flores. She didn't look old enough to have a kid Lauren's age, but she had mentioned a stepdaughter. I'd have to ask Marshall. "We'll see."

"I hate it when you say that."

I handed her the cinnamon-roll bag. "Tough. Eat."

She sighed heavily but took one of the gooey rolls out. "Carmita's?"

"Nope. Piggly Wiggly." I didn't want to tell Lauren just yet about Carmita and Granddad. "Go get dressed. Your dad will be here in thirty minutes. What are y'all doing today?"

She shrugged and took a bite out of her cinnamon roll. "I don't know. We might go swimming at the YMCA. They have a new indoor pool."

Jamie said, "That sounds nice. You should go, too, Rachael. Would be good for you." She winked. "Could be fun, too. I'm sure Marshall wouldn't let you sink."

"Jamie!" I whapped her on the shoulder. "Yeah, I'd look real sexy in shorts and a T-shirt. He'd probably drown me himself."

I had no swimsuit. No swimsuit for a swimming pool, much less for a hot tub. A vision of Nick Rittenour filled my mind, lounging along the side of the hot tub, wine glass in one hand, his naked chest visible above the bubbly water, steam hovering over the surface— Oh, my. My resolve to break the date dissolved completely.

Jamie broke into my trance. "Hey, don't you have to be at Malik's at eight?"

I started. "What? Oh, heck. Yeah. Give me a minute, and I'll get ready."

As I got dressed I realized Nick would see my shot-up leg. It wasn't a pretty sight, but I guess I'd have no choice. Not unless I could find an old-fashioned swimsuit to cover me up from chin to ankle. Wouldn't that be attractive, I thought with a shake of my head.

"You ready yet?" Jamie called out. "Marshall's here to pick up Lauren already."

Good. I didn't want Lauren here alone, waiting. I'd just have to ask Marshall later about getting Jamie some relief. I grabbed my crutches and headed out of the room. "Yes, I'm ready. And Jamie, can I ask a question?"

"Sure."

"That car of yours doesn't go over fifty, does it?"

The ride to Malik's was quick but painless. Jamie, an excellent driver, was careful to avoid the bad roads and high rates of speed, having mercy on my pitiful condition. I was about to get out, when I remembered something. "Oh, heck, I forgot. You don't have to pick me up."

She frowned. "Why not?"

I hesitated, not really wanting to tell Jamie about Nick just yet. Heck, I wasn't even sure about him myself. "I've got to go sign my statement. One of the deputies is going to pick me up here and take me to the sheriff's office."

"You sure? I could drop you by there."

"Positive. I'll see you tomorrow, okay?"

She looked pensive for a moment, then nodded. "Well, okay."

"Why don't you go do something fun for a while? See some friends?"

She shrugged and threw her car out of park. "Everyone's gone or at work. I'll just go home. Mom needs me, anyway."

I watched as she drove off. Poor kid definitely needed a break.

"You coming in, or are you hoping I won't see you out here?"

I turned and smiled. Sporting gray sweats and looking as if he'd just finished his own workout, Malik stood, arms folded, propping open the door.

"Don't worry," I said. "I know the price for skipping class." I followed him down the hallway and into the main therapy room, noting no other victims had arrived yet. I tried to ease up onto one of the tables, failing miserably. I slid back to the floor with a hiss.

"Come on, sport. Up you go." Malik helped me up onto the table and lifted my hands. He shook his head, lips pressed tight. "Rachael! Your hands look like raw meat. I should've noticed yesterday. There's some great stuff my dad used to use—"

"I know, I know. For cow teats."

He laughed. "You got it. Whatever works. Let's get going."

Malik unfastened my brace, and I gritted my teeth as he eased it off. I stared at the angry, three-inch, red scar down the side of my knee. And the matching one-inch-long one.

"It looks terrible, doesn't it?" I muttered.

He shook his head. "On the contrary. It's healing nicely."

"Then why does it still hurt so much?"

He flexed my knee gently, but I still grimaced.

"You were shot, Rachael."

I smirked. "I know that."

He rolled his eyes. "What I mean is, for a rebuilt knee, it's doing just fine." He rubbed his hand over his short-cropped hair. "I talked to your doc yesterday."

"Oh?"

"We're gonna put you in something more lightweight today. Think you'll be more comfortable."

"Anything would be an improvement."

He bent over my leg, gently examining the healing scars. He was nice enough not to comment on my stubbles. I needed to get Lauren to shave my leg for me again.

"Definitely looking better," he commented. "Time to start putting more weight on it."

"Lovely."

"Heard about Stanley. Any news?"

I sighed. "No, I haven't heard anything this morning."

"Heard they'd pulled in Hogey."

"I haven't had a chance to talk to him yet about that. I did talk to Granddad, though. Malik, did your dad ever mention that Carmita and my granddad were in love?"

He chuckled. "Sure he did. Told me years ago. Well. At least a year or so ago."

"Why didn't you tell me?"

He lifted my leg, forcing me to lie back. As he gently flexed it again, with more force this time, I clenched my teeth.

"Dad wasn't sure if Carmita and your granddad even realized it. He figured they'd find the right time, eventually."

"Well, he was right. They got married yesterday, on top of a mountain. On skis."

Malik chuckled and moved to the end of the table. He reached underneath and pulled out a light ankle weight and strapped it around my ankle.

"Lift. How about that—love was right beneath their noses all these years. You know," he said, lifting his arms high, "love will always find a way. Imagine, two lonely souls, searching aimlessly for companionship—"

"Malik. If you break out in song, I'm going to kick you with this thing." I laid my head back and covered my face with my hands. "I can't believe it, though, when it comes right down to it. It's crazy."

He looked at me pointedly. "Is it? So, how's Marshall doing?"

I dropped my hands to my side and growled, "Marshall's just the same as always. Drives me nuts."

"So I hear."

"What did you hear?"

"Leg lifts. Come on."

"You're avoiding my question."

"Just wondering if you had another reason to come back to town besides taking a well-deserved holiday."

Some holiday. I peered at Malik, scrutinizing his face. Then it occurred to me. "Tell Nick Rittenour that no, Marshall has nothing to do with my reasons for being here."

He spread his hands wide. "Hey, it wasn't him wondering. Well, not really."

"Who then?"

"Your granddad."

"Oh. Why didn't—"

"And your aunt, and just about everybody who knows you were coming back for a while."

I frowned. "I told Lauren not to say anything to Marshall, but she did. Why does anybody care about me, anyway?"

Malik rolled his eyes. "This is Saddle Gap, honey. Gossip is the second most popular hobby, next to fishing. And, what with Pamela back, too. . . ." He shrugged.

"I feel like screaming." I thumped the table. "Malik, I'm here to get away from San Antonio for a while. That's all. Well," I said with an exasperated sight, "that and·now, I guess, find out who killed Stanley. But then I'm going back home. I couldn't care less about Marshall. Or Pamela. Did you happen to know him? Stanley, I mean."

"I did." The anger-tinged female voice drifted from behind a curtain separating me and Malik from the rest of the room. I looked at Malik in question. He raised his index finger, then walked over to the curtain and pulled it aside.

"Fine morning to you, Mrs. Halloran."

On the other table sat a woman who, I guessed, was about 55. Years of harsh sunlight had turned her skin leathery brown, but keen blue eyes peered fiercely through thin, bleached-out bangs. She'd twisted what little hair she had into a limp bun at the back of her neck.

She wore a pale yellow outfit at least a size too large. Bony shoulders showed through the thin tank top, her spindly legs stretched out like brown sticks from beneath knee-length shorts. One foot was encased in a white plastic brace.

"Fine morning? Like hell it is. Hello, there," she said, nodding at me.

"Hello," I said.

"Malik, get this damn thing off of me." She gestured toward the brace. "I been waiting for two hours, sitting here forgotten."

Malik nodded and, with more patience than I would have, eased the brace off the woman's leg. "Yes, ma'am, Mrs. Halloran. You're early today. Your appointment wasn't until 8:30."

"All right, all right. I just been sitting here ten minutes. No reason to get your knickers all in a twist. Blasted son will probably forget me. I'll have to sit here all day, just waiting. You don't even have no decent magazines." She eyed me. "Read the new *Glamour*? Great article on that new stuff. Takes out wrinkles." She squinted at me again and pursed her lips. "You could use it, chickie."

Malik chuckled. "I'll call you a cab if Carter forgets you again, Mrs. Halloran. Don't worry."

"Lacey. I always tell you to call me Lacey. But, no, you just go on with that Mrs. Halloran crap. I ain't been a missus in years. Done buried that good-for-nothing-thief boy of mine's good-for-nothing father ten years ago. And that wasn't long enough ago." She nodded to me. "You're Rachael Grant, ain't you?"

"Yes, ma'am."

"The cop that got shot all up? Hell, you should've let 'em chop your leg off."

I looked askance at Malik. He winked.

Oblivious, she rambled on. "Be far easier than putting up with this crazy man and his newfangled torture devices." She looked thoughtful for a moment, then whispered, loud enough for folks in the next room to hear, "Maybe we should strap him there. You think? Give 'im a taste of his own medicine." She gestured toward Malik.

I laughed, but she appeared to be at least partly serious.

"All gruff, no bite," Malik said with a grin as he walked over to her.

Lacey Halloran popped him on the arm. "Like hell you say. I've got plenty of bite yet. You ask that Stanley." She barked a laugh. "Course'n it's too late to bite that one. And I say good riddance."

I perked up at that. "What do you know about Stanley Fletcher?"

She snorted. "No good slimeball. That's what he was. He bought Tumbleweeds, didn't he?"

I nodded. "Yes."

"Better have your granddad check them bank notes. He's a scammer, I tell you."

"How's that?"

The woman fell silent. For a long moment she said nothing, then she nodded her head once, as if conferring with an unseen partner. She snapped around to stare directly at me. Anger flashed in her eyes, and her hands shook with controlled rage.

"He ruined her. Ruined my sister, Bethy." She shook a finger at me. "He don't think I knew about it, but I did. Remember the courthouse, when it burned down?"

I nodded. "Yes, ma'am, I do."

"Well, Bethy's husband, along with a bunch of other folks, were took by Stanley. He was one of them that convinced folks to put in with those investors. Bethy and her husband put all their money in that deal. Lost everything."

Malik said, "I didn't know Stanley was involved with that."

"Just found out myself," I said.

She eyed me again and shook her head. "Long time ago. But it destroyed Bethy's husband and the others involved. 'Stay away from that Stanley Fletcher,' I'd tell my friends. He's no good, I tell you."

I shifted on my table. "Lacey, who were the other investors?"

She fell silent again. I glanced at Malik, saw the concern etched on his face. He leaned over and spoke quietly to the woman. She nodded once, then lay obediently down. Malik drew the curtain between us again, then signaled to one of his assistants to keep Lacey company.

He came back to me, his expression glum. "Best leave her alone now."

"Looks like at least one person hated Stanley enough to kill him."

Malik glanced over his shoulder and rubbed his chin thoughtfully. "Enough to kill him? Probably. But certainly not enough strength."

The image of the woman's thin arms and legs flashed in my mind. "Maybe not. But what about this Bethy? And the other investors?"

"Don't know. You could find out easily enough, though. I never paid much attention to all that."

I poked him in the arm. "Didn't pay much attention to anything back then."

He laughed. "That was during the Annette stage, wasn't it." He shook his head and stared at the floor, but he was smiling. "Wonder whatever happened to her," he mumbled.

"Last I heard, she's been divorced three times and has six kids."

His eyes widened. "You're yanking me."

"Nope."

"Hmm. Going to tell Nick about this?"

Would I tell him about Lacey Halloran? Nope. I did intend to look into what she said, however. I said nothing.

Malik got the hint. "I think we'd best get to work, Lieutenant. You've already wasted precious time. Now, let's go. Lift that leg!"

I obeyed. Thanks to a short surge of adrenaline and two sets of twenty, I was soon drenched. Tears mingled with the sweat, but, thankfully, Malik didn't notice. Or more likely, didn't say anything.

Why did it still hurt so bad? Enough time had passed since I got shot. It shouldn't be so hard. I dropped my leg down, wincing with the pain. "I can't do any more."

"Don't say *can't* around me. One more set."

I tried to lift my leg but it wouldn't budge. Flat-out refused. "I can't do it."

Malik slapped his hands down on the table, making me jump. "Can't or won't?"

I stared at him, in shock. "What is that supposed to mean?"

"You have to try, Rachael."

"I am trying."

"Harder. This isn't going to be easy, getting you back out there. That *is* what you want, isn't it?"

I pulled myself up to my elbows. "Of course it is," I hissed.

"Then prove it, Lieutenant. Lift!"

"Have I told you I hate you?"

He bent over and rubbed my head. "Not today. Now get going."

I managed eight more teeny tiny leg lifts before collapsing. I glared at Malik, waiting for him to yell at me again. "That's all I can do."

"Then let's go to the machines."

"Machines?"

He pointed toward the door. I grabbed my crutches and swung past him, fighting the urge to smack him. Malik walked past me. Ignoring him, I headed toward the bicycles.

"Wrong way, Lieutenant. This way."

I paused, staring at Malik. He stood in front of several gleaming machines that were usually reserved for the high school athletes to tackle. *Certainly he doesn't intend for me to— No way.*

"Yes, way."

"How'd you know what I was thinking?"

"Rachael, take a look at yourself in the mirror there." He pointed to a wall-length mirror I usually ignored. But I looked. He was right—I'd paled visibly, and my eyes were wide with horror.

"Don't worry. You'll be fine." He walked over and stood next to a machine that made me feel faint. He patted it. "This is Harvey."

"You name your machines?"

"Course we do. That way you can yell at them, not us. Let me show you how this works."

I watched in disbelief as Malik hopped onto the seat, stretched out his long, muscular legs, and settled them into two contraptions that reminded me of my last visit to the gyno's office.

"No way."

"Yes, way." He spread his legs, then squeezed them together, weights on cables shooting up in the air behind him. Back and forth, back and forth. Thank God he had on long bicycle shorts. Still, it was quite a sight.

I stared down at my own attire and gulped. Several people entered the room and glanced toward him and back again.

"This will strengthen those outer muscles. Your hamstrings have gotten flabby. And you need to start walking on your leg. Not hopping. Now, let's go."

"I am not getting on that thing."

He jumped off, walked over to me, and took my crutches away. I very reluctantly began to hop over.

"Walk!"

Wincing with every fiery step, I limped over to the machine. Malik adjusted it and changed the weights, then pushed me onto the seat.

"This is embarrassing," I muttered.

"It's gonna get you back out there, Lieutenant. Let's go."

He picked up my good leg and plunked it into place. I felt my bottom lip quiver. He placed my hands around two grips that resembled bicycle handlebars.

I held on for dear life. "This is mortifying."

He picked up my other leg and settled it into position, then moved out of the way. "Okay, now push your legs together."

For a moment nothing happened. I pushed, nearly screaming with the agony. I threw my head back, closed my eyes, and, with a most unladylike grimace, finally managed to get my legs together.

"Good! Now, do it again, Rachael."

I relaxed, and my legs smacked back into open position again. With monumental effort, I managed one more. Then another.

Sweat poured into my eyes, and my hands shook, I gripped so hard. I no longer cared if anyone watched. It hurt like hell, but he was right—I could feel muscles I hadn't felt in weeks respond to the torture.

"Damn you, Malik!" I opened my eyes and screamed. My legs shot apart.

A man dressed in black shorts and a sleeveless gray sweatshirt stood in the doorway, his arms crossed, an appreciative grin plastered on his face.

Oh, no. No. Not Nick Rittenour.

"Hey. Got here early," he said. And then the blasted man winked.

Chapter 8

"MALIK. DARLING. If you know what's good for you, you'll get me out of this thing." I shot him my best cop glare. "Now."

He obeyed. With his help, I eased to my feet.

"You could have warned me," I hissed, but he chuckled and said, "And ruin all the fun?"

"I hate you, hate you, hate you."

"Didn't know he was here for you, anyway. Should've told me you were expecting company."

I elbowed him in the ribs as I limped slowly past. Nick unfolded his arms but didn't move toward me as I made my painful journey. I gave him a go-to-hell look, just for good measure. Then I crooked a finger at my therapist. "Malik, where's my brace."

"You're not done yet, Lieutenant. Whirlpool."

I shook my head. "No time for whirlpools. I have things to do."

"And you can start them in the whirlpool," Malik said, herding me toward the appropriate room.

I tried to shove past him, but the man was as solid as a cement truck. "Come on, Malik. I need to go."

Nick approached, his expression grim. "We need to talk, Rachael."

Great. Malik pushed inside the room. Fortunately, no one else was inside. He turned on the whirlpool machine and motioned for me to follow.

I eased up onto the edge of the tub and reluctantly plunked my leg in.

"Mind if I talk to Rachael alone?" Nick asked.

"No problem." Malik nodded at me as he left, closing the door behind him.

I looked at Nick and said, "How come I get the feeling I'm not going to like this?"

"You won't. An investigator has been assigned to the case."

I frowned. "Who?"

Nick rubbed his chin with his hand. "Woman by the name of Babette Boone."

I burst out laughing. "What a horrible name. Poor woman."

He shrugged, but he was grinning. "Graduated with my brother Tom. She's tough and doesn't like people digging into her business."

I sighed. "I detect another warning in there." I shifted on the tub's rim. The hot bubbly water felt heavenly, and I longed to sink my entire body inside.

"Not exactly a warning."

"A 'gentle' request then?" I leaned against the wall and closed my eyes, grateful for the support. This morning's workout had been extra stressful, and my shoulders still felt tied up in knots.

I opened my eyes. Nick moved to the left side of the whirlpool, which was high enough that he could lean on it and look up at me. My gaze kept shifting to his face.

This was really the first good, close look I'd had of the man since the day before at Tumbleweeds. He still hadn't shaved, and his eyes looked more green today than hazel. His hair was mussed up, too. The classic scruffy look. I liked it. His shirt tag stuck halfway out, and I fought the urge to lean over and tuck it in.

"*Request* is a good way to put it," he said, apparently oblivious to my scrutiny. Or else he just ignored it. Or, maybe, he was enjoying it thoroughly. "Sheriff Rosa told the good detective that you were a cop and had caused a scene."

I bolted upright, nearly getting my wish for full immersion. "Caused a scene? How, I'd like to know?"

Nick smiled, then leaned down and dipped his hand into the bubbles. His hand encountered my foot, and darned if he didn't grab it.

"Careful there."

"Don't worry. Relax."

I eyed him skeptically, then leaned against the wall again.

He began to massage the bottom of my foot, and I purred. "That feels wonderful."

"Got to take care of your feet, Rachael. Being on crutches doesn't mean you aren't getting foot stress."

"Foot stress?"

He nodded, then gestured for my other foot. I gladly obliged. "Foot stress. In Saudi Arabia I learned that lesson well. Walking on sand is tough work."

"Saudi Arabia? When were you there?"

"Desert Storm."

I swallowed. I knew a couple of cops who'd served there. Some of the things they saw during that brief foray were horrendous.

Now wasn't the time to ask Nick, however. He removed his hand and dried it on a towel, then leaned against the tub, staring into nothing. He abruptly shook his head and smiled, though it didn't reach his eyes.

If I'd known him better, I would have asked what he was thinking about. Instead, I said, "What's happened on the case, Nick? What have they found out so far? Or can I ask that. They haven't arrested anyone, have they?"

"No, no one's been arrested. So many different fingerprints were lifted from the scene, they aren't going to be much help."

"Not surprising. What about the coroner? Anything there?"

"Not yet. I expect to hear from Marisol any time now, though."

"Any background of interest on Stanley?"

"I'm sure the detective is taking care of that."

My shoulders sank, and I stared into the swirling bubbles. The silence hung between us. I was starting to feel a little frustrated, even though only a scant twenty-four hours had passed since the body had been discovered.

A feeling of disenchantment started to push at me. I was being forced into a position I was all too familiar with—a non-participatory spectator role. The other time I'd been in this position still reeked of freshness.

It had started about halfway through my long-running pursuit of Fernando. More than once, I had been warned by my sergeant I was a cop, not a detective, and to concern myself with my beat and not the local drug lord. I had accepted that at first and played by the rules. But it hadn't been until I secretly took on investigating the matter on my own time that any headway in the case was made.

Only Dave knew how much extra time I'd spent tracking the bastard. And only Dave knew I was to blame for my injury. If I'd followed proper procedure, turning over all my hard-won findings to Detective Litch, I might have escaped Fernando's wrath.

And he might be sitting in jail now, instead of running around San Antonio and threatening me. All my notes on the case were still at home, useless to me now, and definitely of no use to Litch.

I grimaced. Litch would have had me tossed in the slammer if he'd ever found my file on Fernando. As it was, everyone but Dave thought my encounter with the gang leader was an unhappy coincidence. Unfortunately it wasn't. And Fernando was angry with me. Very angry. I'd had no choice but to leave San Antonio while I was still laid up and defenseless.

And now here I was in a similar position once again. Forced to sit on the sidelines. I didn't like it one bit. Yet I'd more or less already promised I'd keep out of the investigation into Stanley Fletcher's death.

I wouldn't be able to keep my word, I feared.

Crossing one arm across my stomach, I peered at Nick through half-closed eyes. "Why else does that woman's name sound so familiar? The investigator. It's not from school, either."

Nick grinned. "She routed out Elkins Ledbetter. Put Saddle Gap on the map of Texas for all of five seconds."

I raised my eyebrows in surprise. "Now I remember. The poodle case."

"That's the one. Made her, um, famous."

"And she's who they assigned to this case?" *Great.*

"Yes, ma'am. Indeed she is."

Elkins Ledbetter was a wanna-be serial killer who specialized in kidnapping prize pooches. At first the disappearances had been mostly ignored—or chalked up as coyote activity.

But after the tenth or so reported incident—which involved a local celebrity teacup poodle, Champion Hot Smokin' Sassafras—the sheriff's office had become involved.

They were stumped. Then in poured Babette Boone. She solved the case—and, the experts claimed, just in time. In Elkins's desk drawer were plans to toss the puppies aside and pursue people, instead.

Hot Smokin' was recovered. People had been more up in arms over the dogs then than they apparently were now over Stanley.

Since that case, as far as I knew, Detective Boone hadn't been back to Saddle Gap. Until now. My discontent flamed into frustration. "Whose great idea was this, anyway?"

"Not Rosa's."

I snorted. "No doubt when the news media swoops down on Saddle Gap once again, he'll be standing right by the detective's side."

Nick's eyes narrowed. "The important thing is to find the killer, Rachael."

I nodded, chagrined. "I know, I know. But I don't like being told to stay out of it."

"Neither do I."

I looked at him in surprise. "You don't?"

He shrugged. "I have a feeling that telling you to stay out of something will make you do just the opposite."

"Wouldn't you? Especially with half my relatives as suspects?"

The corner of his mouth lifted the tiniest bit. "Just grant me a favor, will you?"

"What's that?"

"Keep me informed about what you ferret out."

I hesitated. I appraised Deputy Rittenour. In his extreme casual mode, he still looked the part of the policeman. Shoulders back, keenly aware of his surroundings. His back to a blank wall, not the door.

The sounds filtering from outside the room didn't escape his notice. I had a feeling I wouldn't be able to hide anything from this man, even though, as a fellow cop, I pretty much understood how he ticked.

"All right. Deal," I agreed. "If I find anything, I'll let you know."

He nodded once. "Good. Now, where did you need to go?"

Reaching into my back pocket, I whipped out my little notebook and pen. I waved it in front of him, then flipped the cover open. "I have a list."

"Thorough."

Smiling, I nodded. "First, I want to go to my grandfather's house."

"By the way, your grandfather called the station this morning. Said Carmita was with him."

I sighed. "Yes, but did he tell you she didn't fly up with him?"

He frowned. "I'm not sure. What did he tell you?"

"That she went to tell her sons first."

"About what?"

"They got married."

"How do you feel about that?"

I shrugged. "He sounded happy, Nick. But I don't know. Like you said, I don't know that much about her." I tapped my nose with the pen. "Maybe she paid someone to do it."

He nodded once, but his eyes twinkled. "Possible."

"That's why I want to go to the house. Maybe we'll find—"

Nick raised a hand and looked at the door. "Someone's coming."

"Malik, probably."

The door opened and Malik poked his head in. "Done yet? Rachael, waddle on in here, and let's get you fixed up with this new brace."

"Waddle? I don't waddle. I glide."

Nick was seized by a coughing fit. Ignoring him and Malik, I eased out of the tub, grabbed a towel, and gently dried my leg. I noted Nick's quick examination, raised eyebrow, and quirky grin, and once again I felt chagrin for not having shaved my hurt leg. I tossed the towel in his face.

Before he could retaliate, I walked to the door with all the dignity I could muster. The two jesters followed behind me, showing a brief glimpse of intelligence by not saying a word.

With my leg encased in the new brace, I actually felt somewhat comfortable. Malik would let me have only one crutch, but I thought maybe that would be okay. Hopefully.

Nick was kind enough to drive like a normal human being, and within a few minutes, we were outside Granddad's house.

I'd always loved this place. Built of blocks of limestone gathered from Granddad's oldest brother's quarry "back east," the one-story house stayed incredibly comfortable year-round. A huge cottonwood leaned protectively over the roof, and a cactus garden that my grandmother had designed greeted all visitors with a showy display of blooms.

Under the tree, a freshly painted green swing eased back and forth in the breeze. It wasn't the first one to grace the yard. I'd done my fair share of necking with Marshall on its predecessor. I scooted past the swing and the uncomfortable memories.

Privet hedges lined either side of the property, blocking off the house from the next-door neighbors, except for a small gap on either side. Granddad had always been the type to care about his neighbors, and they about him. Lots of talking over late-night cups of coffee had taken place in those gaps.

Though spring had barely sprung, already his small defiant patch of lawn had greened up, and the last remnants of daffodils waved merrily in the breeze. I remember when I was just a little girl Grandmother would plant them; and later, when I moved in with my grandparents, I remember she would hand me the scissors to cut several to take to my schoolteachers. Granddad always swore they wouldn't grow in this part of Texas, but Grandmother ignored him, proving him wrong every year.

I reached into my fanny pack and pulled out my Swiss Army knife, cutting a few of the last blooms. Nick followed me into the house. A huge fly zipped past us, making a beeline toward the bedrooms.

Inside, the only sound came from the study, where Granddad's clock collection ticked away in a rhythmic chorus. Deep tones, light tones, gentle tick-tocks, and the mechanical clink of his German cuckoos accompanied my steps across the wooden floors. I took a few moments to wind those that needed it.

Nick joined me, and for a few moments we worked in silence. I watched him from the corner of my eye as he reached on top of the grandfather clock for its key, inserted it in the case, then expertly wound it up.

He caught me looking and smiled. "My dad has one of these," he said, running his hand down the clock's wooden side. "Not as nice as this one."

I moved closer to him, appreciating his appreciation, and said, "My parents bought this for him when they were in England."

His head snapped toward me. "Isn't that where—"

I nodded, fighting back the clumped-up feeling in my throat. "Yes. That's where my parents died. They beat that clock back here. It was strange, knowing they were gone, getting one last present from them."

I sank onto a tapestry-covered chair, automatically plumping up the pillows. "It arrived while we were gone to the funeral. They'd written a letter and sent it with the clock. For a long time, my grandparents kept the clock boxed away in the storage room, but one day I discovered it. I insisted they bring it out and set it up as my dad had intended. I think I began to heal the day Granddad first turned the key and I heard those chimes."

"I'm sorry about your loss, Rachael."

I looked up at him. "Thank you. I still miss them a lot."

"What did you want to do here?"

I pushed myself out of the chair and hobbled toward the bedrooms on the east side of the house. "I don't know. I just wanted to look, I guess."

"Holler if you need me."

"'kay."

I peered first into the guest room. The blasted fly had made its way in here. I waved my hand at it in annoyance, but it zipped off again. I took in the neatly made bed, the Spartan but comfortable furnishings.

Last time I'd been here, there was nothing remarkable about the room. Now Carmita's things occupied the premises.

Her sewing basket. A small frame with a half-finished sampler in a corner. On the floral chintz couch, stacks of cookbooks perched neatly on the edge, even more on the floor. On the wall over the couch hung a beautiful Indian blanket, salsa reds and sunny yellows woven with midnight black. The room had become Carmita's haven. So much happening right beneath my nose, and I hadn't even known.

I sniffed, suddenly aware of a strange odor, and shuffled on into Granddad's room.

I stopped short.

The fly flew past me and buzzed around the room in lazy circles. I watched, transfixed, as it spiraled down, finally coming to join its mates on a man sitting, legs sprawled, arms akimbo, on my grandfather's bedroom chair.

The man's mouth hung open, his gaze glued to some horror on the wall behind me. I covered my mouth and took a step backward. It was the straw-colored hair and the Grateful Dead T-shirt that gave away his identity.

My cousin Hogey.

A strangled cry ripped from my throat. I hurled myself toward the bathroom, collapsed on the floor, and promptly tossed my breakfast, only vaguely aware that Nick was shouting my name.

Chapter 9

A COOL, WET CLOTH gently bathed the back of my neck. I groaned. "I can't believe I did that."

"Don't worry about it. Here." Nick handed me the cloth, then helped me up off the floor.

I flushed the toilet and glanced at my reflection in the mirror. Red-rimmed eyes centered in a deathly pale face stared back at me. "I'm losing it."

"Anybody would. You didn't expect it."

I shook my head. "But that's just it, Nick. I should have—" I buried my face in the cool cloth, then jerked on the faucet and dropped the cloth on the side of the sink. Yanking open a drawer, I pulled out a half-used tube of toothpaste and quickly scrubbed my teeth, using my index finger.

He watched me, arms crossed, a speculative expression on his face. "You should've what?" he said after I rinsed out my mouth.

Bracing myself on the edge of the sink, I looked up at Nick. But he surprised me. Before I could speak, he touched my lips with his finger and shook his head. "Looks like he's been dead for a while, Rachael. There was no way to know he'd be next."

"Next," I responded dully. "Guess that means he didn't kill Stanley, huh."

"Stay here a second, and I'll go get someone up here."

I didn't answer. He left the bathroom, and I eased myself up onto the countertop and leaned against the towel cabinet. The damp washcloth was in the sink, but I didn't have the energy to pick it up. I blanked my mind and closed my eyes, forcing all sorts of nasty thoughts to take a hike. I could feel little beads of sweat pop out on my forehead and make my shirt cling to my skin. My nerves were shot, my brain soggy as oatmeal. I forced my thoughts back out on another hike, fervently wishing they'd stay put.

From the kitchen, Nick's conversation drifted out where I could hear him. Short. Quick. To the point. No reason to hurry, just like with Stanley. Hogey was definitely dead, and there was no way to help him.

But why? Why was he dead? Where was his car? Why wasn't he at the guest ranch? *Oh, Hogey. What knowledge did you die with? What got you killed?*

I thought back to the day before, to the fear I'd seen in Hogey's eyes. Now I knew he had other reasons to look scared, besides the obvious.

Nick walked back in. I opened my eyes just enough to watch him. His presence in the small bathroom was comforting. He rinsed out the washcloth and, with welcome tenderness, wiped my face and then eased the cloth around the back of my neck.

"You up to a better look? I want you to see something."

I nodded. Easing off the counter, I followed him back into the room. I did a quick scan, avoiding looking at my cousin. Nothing seemed out of place. The bed was smooth and untouched, no doubt as Granddad had left it. Hogey's shoes sat to the side of the bed. A can of Shiner Bock sat on the bedside table. Granddad didn't drink the stuff, so I knew it had to be Hogey's.

Then I looked at my cousin. This time I was ready, but still my stomach roiled. I took a tentative step forward. Nick walked to the left of me and crouched down. He stared intently at Hogey, and I could almost see the mental list he was making. I took a deep breath and started the same mental notations.

No socks, shoes by the bed. Hogey's worn brown corduroy jeans were unbuttoned, the zipper partially down. His gut rolled over too-tight pants. A stream of dark blood ran down his belly, soaking into his crotch. An arrow was perfectly centered in the *E* in the word *Dead* of his T-shirt.

I looked away, feeling my stomach begging to betray me once again. "It's always such a shock," I whispered.

I glanced at Nick. He stood, then reached out and touched my shoulder. "I understand."

I shook my head. "No, you don't understand what I mean."

He considered me for a moment, then said, "What do you mean?"

"It's always such a shock," I said again, this time in a sing-song voice. "That's what a paramedic told me the first time I saw a murder victim. But he was wrong." Tears blurred my eyes. I wrapped my arms around myself, nearly losing my crutch.

"It was a shock the first time—and even the third. But soon, too soon, a dead body was just another dead body to me." I took a deep breath and let it out in a shudder.

"I've seen so many, Nick. Kids who've overdosed on crack. Teenagers who've run across a bad batch of heroine. Elderly people, afraid of high electric bills, who've fried to death in their own homes for fear of turning on their air conditioners. I lost the shock, Nick. All those dead bodies weren't people to me anymore. I was immune to the pain. Even after Fernando."

"Who's Fernando?"

"The man who wants to kill me." My voice caught. "I knew from our first encounter he intended to win the war I'd started. But even then, I tucked my real feelings away. Hid it behind my damn stoic façade. 'Can't let them see you crack, Lieutenant Grant.' I should've been scared, but I wasn't." I tore my gaze away from Hogey. "No, I couldn't let myself think like this. What was I becoming?"

"You were coping, Rachael. That's all."

"Coping, like a robot." I leaned on my crutch, grateful for its support. "Cope or crack." I took a deep breath and smiled weakly at Nick. "I think maybe I've stopped coping."

I turned and went to the living room, where the comforting tick-tock of the freshly wound clocks beckoned me. I sat down on the same chair I'd sat on before. I knew the investigation team would look for prints all over the house. Mine would be limited to the front room, bathroom, and whatever I didn't remember touching in the bedroom.

Nick followed me, but after a quick squeeze of my shoulder, he opened the front door and walked out onto the porch.

I was grateful for the chance to pull myself together. For a long moment I sat, numb, forcing myself to think as I stared at the grandfather clock's face. Who, why, and what next? What next, for I knew beyond doubt that whatever was going on wasn't over yet.

Fifteen slow, agonizing minutes passed before the sounds of sirens wailed in the distance. Nick poked his head inside, his concerned gaze falling on me. "You okay?" A fly zoomed through the open door. My stomach burned.

"Yeah. I guess."

"Babette's here."

No sooner had he spoken than Investigator Babette Boone trudged in. I started in surprise as she filled the doorway. I don't know what I was expecting—something resembling a gorilla, maybe?

Detective Boone's keen blue eyes cut to me for a split second, then her gaze darted about the room. All the while she nodded, her blonde helmet hair budged not a millimeter. Her face, florid from excitement or exertion or who knew what, was free of any makeup. Short, sausage legs were stuffed into army fatigues, which in turn were laced into combat boots. A crisp white shirt topped the unusual attire. She stood at about five foot two. With drill sergeant precision, she commanded the troops to begin their work.

Then she abruptly turned to me. "Lieutenant Grant. Babs Boone."

Using the chair as support, I extended my hand. "Rachael, please."

She nodded briskly, taking in my leg. "What a shame. Let's go check out the corpse."

She whirled on her heel and marched toward Hogey, her combat boots striking the wooden floor and shaking the entire house. I glanced at Nick, but he studiously ignored me.

By the time I made it into the bedroom, Investigator Boone had come to a standstill in front of Hogey. Hands on spread knees, she looked him in the eye. The stench and buzzing flies didn't deter her from poking once at Hogey's chest.

"Yep. He's dead, alright. You move anything?"

I shook my head then said, "No."

"Touch anything?"

"In the front room. The clocks." I paused. "And the bathroom. The sink and toilet."

She peered at me over her shoulder. "Sure is revolting, isn't it."

I didn't say anything, but she didn't seem to notice.

Boone straightened, then spoke quietly to the two technicians who had begun their work. They kept glancing, wild-eyed, at Hogey. I wondered if this was only the second body they'd ever actually tended to. Both looked to be barely out of high school. Their heads bobbed in eager unison as she gave them her instructions.

She clapped them on the back and nodded her head in satisfaction. "Go to it, boys. Don't disappoint me."

"Yes, Inspector," they chimed.

Boone threw her head back and laughed. "*Inspector!* Ain't that a riot?" She was still laughing as she tromped back down the hallway. "Come on, Rachael, Deputy Rittenour. Let's go out to my car and have a nice little chat and see if we can't make some sort of sense out of this mess."

I eyed Nick, who shrugged. "She's not exactly what I expected," I said.

We made our way outside in silence. Each room we passed was filled with technicians dusting for fingerprints and taking samples from the garbage, the sink, the floor. A cup here, a bottle there, including the beer bottle from Granddad's room. A much more thorough investigation than the one at Tumbleweeds, I thought.

Investigator Boone leaned against a white Ford Bronco, hands perched on her hips. She watched my slow movement across the lawn. Any second I expected her to grab a whistle and blow it at me to pick up the pace.

Visions of drill at the police academy filled my mind. As an older recruit, and a mom to boot, the first few weeks of physical activity at the academy had been pure agony. Only sheer stubbornness had forced my body into shape. Boone glared at me. The hairs at the back of my neck prickled as I remembered similar stares from disapproving sergeants.

But this wasn't boot camp, I reminded myself, and this woman was merely the investigator assigned to the case. I raised my chin and moved faster. Nick walked beside me, matching my pace, a mere stroll for him.

A clipboard sat on the hood of the Bronco, a wad of well-thumbed papers tucked inside the clip. They blew in the breeze, which felt delicious on my skin. I had to fight not to gulp in the fresh air. I hadn't realized how stale Granddad's house was. Worse than stale.

One of the technicians ran up with a lawn chair and popped it open. Detective Boone motioned for me to sit.

"Thanks."

"Need your wits about you. How long's it been?" She pointed to my leg with her clipboard.

"Almost three weeks."

"Ouch a shame."

I suddenly wondered if there was another reason besides a flash of kindness for getting me the chair. I was forced to look up into her appraising eyes.

The deputy who brought the chair cleared his throat. I recognized him. Paul something, a classic good ol' boy. "Uh, Rachael?" he said.

"Hi, Paul. Thanks for the chair."

He blushed. "You're welcome. Um, do you mind if I ask you something?"

Boone said, "We're conducting an investigation here, Pickup."

That was it. Paul Pickup. I smiled. "Sure, go ahead."

"Will you be running Tumbleweeds? I've got off in a couple weekends, and I was wanting to take my son and a few of his friends down the river. Maybe do some fishing."

"You have a son? How old is he?" I asked.

Paul grinned and straightened up proudly. "Six years old. His name is Brandon. Think you'll be opening up again?"

I shook my head. "I don't know, Paul. I'll look into it." I glanced meaningfully at the detective. "I haven't been given the clear yet. I don't even know what the status of it is."

His face fell. "Oh. Well, I hope you open it up, Rachael. We sure would miss the place. Why, last year I shot the biggest buck of the season! You should see it. Your grandfather put it on the Glory Wall. That was your idea, wasn't it?"

I smiled in pleasure. "Yes, it was. Thank you."

"Is that all, Pickup?" Boone barked. "We're not here for idle chitchat. You can talk about blasting Bambi later."

Paul's mouth clamped shut, and he stared at the investigator. I think he'd actually forgotten she was there. Poor guy. He skittered off, looking over his shoulder as if the devil were after him.

I looked at Investigator Boone. For a long moment she didn't say a word, then she glanced at her clipboard and tapped it with one pink fingernail. The immaculate manicure surprised me. I'd expected gnawed stubs.

She gestured to Nick. "All right, Deputy. Since you were a witness to this little incident, too, I'd like you to step aside for a bit. I'll talk to you in a minute."

Nick left me with a reassuring glance. Despite being outside and surrounded by about twenty people, I felt remarkably alone with Detective Boone.

"Now," she went on. "Tell me exactly what happened."

I nodded. "Nick and I arrived at the house shortly after ten. My grandfather is out of town, so I thought I'd come by and wind his clocks for him. They damage easily if not wound daily."

I was careful not to pause as I went on. I wasn't ready to tell the detective the real reason I was there. It occurred to me, then, I hadn't had a chance to scrounge around the house any. I would have to come back later and see what I could discover on my own. Somehow I'd have to get back over here by myself.

"Nick and I wound all the clocks. This took approximately five minutes. After we were done, I proceeded down the hallway to my grandfather's room. He has two cuckoo clocks in there that needed winding. I was partway down the hall when I smelled something. Two seconds later, I discovered what it was."

"Next?"

I paused. My cheeks flushed and I swallowed. I glanced up

at the detective. "I immediately retreated to the bathroom and threw up."

She nodded once. "What a shame. Anything else to add?"

I shook my head. "No."

"When did you last enter the premises?"

"A year ago."

She frowned. "Who else has keys to this place?"

I shrugged. "Carmita did. I don't know who else would."

"What about your cousin? Would he have had a key?"

I immediately stiffened. "I don't know. Hogey worked for Granddad, so he might."

"What did he do?"

"He took care of the stables and handled all the trail rides. Despite his other shortcomings, he was very good with horses."

"Your granddad have any pets? Any nosy neighbors?"

"No pets here. As for nosy neighbors, I don't know."

"What about this Carmita person. What can you tell me about her?"

The late-morning sun felt hot against my skin. I wished I'd brought the washcloth outside with me, but I'd left it in the bathroom sink. I shook my head. "There isn't much to tell about Carmita. She and my granddad have been working together for years. She does all the cooking at the ranch."

"How long they been a couple?"

I shrugged. "They're married now. That's all I know. You'll have to ask Carmita and my granddad."

"Intend to do just that."

The way she spoke made the hair on the back of my neck rise again. But I relaxed. There was no way she could accuse them; they were still more than half a day away from Saddle Gap, tucked safely away in the mountains. I hoped. At that moment a deputy car drove up, interrupting the "nice little chat."

"Detective Boone," the deputy called out.

"Hold on a second, Grant." She left me sitting in the chair and poked her head inside the car window. She didn't have to bend down much. She gestured with her hand and then walked back toward me, shaking her head. "Found your cousin's car, Ms. Grant."

"Rachael."

She nodded. "On the other side of the river, sticking out of the water."

I looked at her in surprise. "In the river?" Great. Even if they hauled it out, any chance of finding any sort of print would spiral down to nothing.

I collapsed back into the chair and stared at a small yellow flower bursting from the yard. A dandelion. Granddad had always insisted they be left alone, whereas Grandmother had waged war against the weeds for years. Not another dandelion was in sight. I hoped it propagated well.

"Anything else you need to know?" I asked.

"Nope. Unless there's something else you need to tell me."

I decided to take a stab at turning the tables. "Do you have any leads, Detective?"

Her lips pursed into a thin white line. "Guess we can mark Hogey off. I have a few in mind, though. Seems Stanley wasn't much favored in these parts."

"What about the autopsy on Stanley?"

She shrugged, then huffed. "Preliminary report indicates a single shot to the chest, with an arrow. Like your cousin there. Same kind. Not much more than that. Toxicology is still running tests."

"Will you let me know the results?" I asked.

She appraised me for a long moment. "Do me a favor, Ms. Grant. Stay out of this investigation. Let me do my job."

I stood, resuming my towering stance over the other woman. "I hope you will, Detective Boone," I said. "I don't want to cause any problems. But you must understand, I fully intend to help my grandfather any way I can."

She stared up at me, her eyes squinting so they almost disappeared. She finally nodded once, then turned on her heel. "Just remember, Rachael Grant," she called over her shoulder, "to consider yourself. You're my number one suspect, after all."

Chapter 10

NUMBER ONE SUSPECT. The woman was nuts. Nick stayed silent as he drove me back to the cabin. I was grateful we didn't discuss our conversations with Boone. There would be time for that later. All I wanted to do now was crawl inside the air-conditioned house and collapse on the bed.

When he turned into the gravel driveway, I saw a patrol car parked outside beneath the mesquite trees. The deputy waved through his open window and flashed an okay when Nick raised his hand.

Good. All was well here, at least. I felt sorry for the deputy, though. It was only mid-April, but the temperature had climbed to just over ninety degrees.

When Nick pulled to a stop, I placed my hand on the steering wheel. "Don't get out. I'll be fine."

He nodded. "Is five o'clock tomorrow all right?"

"How about four?"

His smile appeared. "Sure. Want to go grocery shopping with me? I need to pick up some fish for tomorrow."

I laughed. "I thought you caught it yourself. You mean we're having store-bought?"

He raised his hands and shrugged. "Never claimed to be a fisherman. Besides, the Rio Grande doesn't have lobster."

Lobster. I closed my eyes in delight. "I haven't had lobster in ages."

"Cop salaries. I understand. This is a special occasion, though."

"Oh?"

"Yeah. Malik lost a bet."

"Oh." I opened the car door. "I don't think I want to know about this, do I?"

He grinned a Cheshire-cat grin. Funny how his eyes sparkled mischievously. I always thought it was impossible to credit eyes with that ability, but with Nick, the description fit perfectly. I eased out of the car and slammed the door shut. "See you at four tomorrow."

He laughed. "All right, four. Rest well."

"Thanks."

His expression grew serious. "And don't worry about the place. The sheriff has promised to keep an eye on things out here."

"Okay, thanks." I paused, feeling suddenly awkward. "I'll talk to you later."

"Sure. I'll call."

He drove off and waved his hand out the open window. I waved back, though I knew he couldn't see me. The moment he was out of sight, I collapsed against the front door.

Good lord, what was I going to do about Nick Rittenour? My heart was all pitter-patter at the thought of seeing him again. I had almost forgotten how wonderfully scary it felt. I hadn't had that pitter-patter feeling since high school. Not since Marshall first glanced my way.

I didn't realize until he was at the foot of the steps that the deputy had gotten out of the car. "Excuse me, Ms. Grant?"

"Rachael," I automatically answered. Then I noticed the package he held. "Is that for me?"

"Yes, ma'am. Delivered a little while ago." He handed me the package, tipped his cowboy hat, and sauntered back to his car.

I checked the label; it was from Dave. My mail. How I wished it had been my Vicodan.

With a heavy groan, I unlocked the door and pushed my way inside. It wasn't until I was about to close the door that I saw Jamie's car approach. She waved at the deputy and popped out of her car, leaving it running. Thank heavens. I needed to rest and didn't feel like talking, and I didn't want to read my mail with an audience. I tossed the package onto the counter and eased back out to the front porch.

She bounded up the steps, a box clutched in her hands. "Hey, girl, you look wiped out."

"I am. You haven't heard?"

She shook her head. "What's up?" She frowned in concern. "Rachael, you okay?"

Now I wasn't so sure. I felt every muscle in my body release. With Jamie, at least, I didn't have to be on pins and needles. "Hogey's dead, Jamie."

She gasped, raising her hand to her mouth. "Oh, no! Rachael, how?"

"Just like Stanley."

She paled. "An arrow. Oh, Rachael, this is awful! What are you going to do?"

"Go take a nap." I pushed the door open. "I'm not sure I can deal with anything else right now."

She followed me in, motioning me to the couch. "There you go," she said, settling me in. "Hold on. I'll be right back." She flew out the front door.

I heard her car shudder to a stop. *That piece of junk needs replacing,* I thought. Marshall drove a brand-new pickup; surely he could help his sister with a new set of wheels.

"You need a new car, Jamie," I said when she came back in. "That thing is older than Lauren."

"Born the same year, actually. Mom likes it." She shook her head and frowned. Her face looked pinched and tired. "I think getting rid of it right now would upset her too much." She straightened and handed me the box she'd been holding. "Present for you."

"Hey, what. . . ." Dumbfounded, I opened the box and gingerly picked up the two bits of bright turquoise. "Um, what is this?"

"A string bikini, silly. I thought about black, but with your coloring, turquoise is much sexier."

"Sexier? Jamie, I can't wear this! My gosh, woman, I've had a kid! I'm not sexy!"

"Bullcorn."

I raised an eyebrow.

"Uh-huh. Look. I nearly forgot. I've brought my stuff with me. How about a makeover?"

With a skeptical eye, I looked at my ex-sister-in-law. "Why?" I asked suspiciously.

"Oh, no reason. Just in case you want to go swimming any-time soon."

Then I remembered. Marshall was taking Lauren swim-ming. I sighed. "Just in case, huh?"

She dropped onto the couch, on her knees. Her face shined with eagerness. "Come on, Rachael. Let me take a whack at your hair."

I touched my head. "I don't know—"

"Come on, I promise I can make you look real sexy."

Sexy? I lifted up a hank of my hair and stared at it. What would Nick think of me with short hair? And in a string bikini, to boot? Oh, my gosh. My face burned at the thought.

Thirty minutes later, my hair had lost at least nine inches. And that wasn't all.

"There. Isn't that fantastic?"

I stared, amazed, at my reflection in the full-length mir-ror. The bikini fit perfectly—not quite as daring as I'd feared. It actually did a decent job of covering everything. I turned slightly and shrieked. Except my butt.

"Jamie, I can't—"

"You can." She turned me around. "There. Now, see? See how the highlights make you look younger?"

She was right. I peered closer at the mirror and smiled. The touches of gray at my temples were now touches of gold. With all the weight gone from my hair, it brushed my shoul-ders in a full bob. It actually had some life.

Jamie shook her head back and forth, and I mimicked her, delighting in the swingy feel. She'd insisted on bangs, promis-ing me that the hippie look of all one hair length had gone out with the Volkswagen. I'd reminded her a new model had come out recently.

"And you're a new model, too, Rachael. Well, an improved model, anyway." She grinned at me in the mirror. "Like?"

I ran my fingers through the new bangs. "Okay. Yes," I said, turning and giving her a hug. "Yes, I like."

"And that bathing suit even gives you cleavage."

"Not something I lack, anyway, Jamie," I said wryly.

She began to scoop up her things. A glance at the clock told her it was already 12:30. "I've got to get going, Rachael.

It's almost time for Mom's medication. Oh, and speaking of medication. Marshall said you lost your Vicodan?"

"Yes. I called to have some sent to Whitmarsh's."

"Let me know when it gets here, and I'll pick it up for you."

I reached out and touched her shoulder, stopping her. "Jamie, honey, thanks. For everything."

She glanced up, a beatific smile filling her face. It edged away the tiredness, and she looked like a young girl again. "You're welcome. Have fun with the haircut, okay?"

"I will." She gave me a quick hug and then I was alone, at long last. I set the alarm clock for two. Ten seconds later, still in my new bathing suit, I collapsed onto the bed.

Thousands of flies flew toward me. They were in my hair, my nose, my mouth. The droning of their wings hurt my ears. I brushed futilely at them, striking out with my hands, trying desperately to stop the incessant ringing sound.

My hand struck something hard, and I bolted up in bed, panting heavily. I stared wide-eyed at my reflection in the mirror. My wild flailing had sent the alarm clock underneath the bed, and it still buzzed merrily away, oblivious to its role in my nightmare. I used the cord to pull it out, then shut the darn thing off. Three o'clock? I could swear I'd set it for two.

I fell back onto the pillows and stared at the ceiling fan and took several deep breaths. My heart still raced, and by the tangle of my bedcovers, I knew I'd had a far worse nightmare than I remembered.

Swinging off of the bed, I made it to the bathroom. I ripped the Velcro tabs apart and slid my leg out of the new brace. This one was much better than the last, which had been like wearing armor. I was glad Jamie had washed my hair before she cut it; it was going to take all my spare time just to shave my legs.

I'd just finished pulling on a pair of shorts and a clean T-shirt when a sharp rap sounded on the front door.

"Just a minute!" I hollered. I grabbed my crutch and half-hopped into the living room. A man was looking through the front window, his hands cupped on either side of his face. I faltered for a moment, then realized it was Marshall.

"Hi," he said as I opened the door.

I looked past him. The deputy still waited patiently out in his car. I had to wonder about Saddle Gap and its obvious abundance of manpower.

"Come on in, Marshall." I headed for the kitchen. There was something comforting about being surrounded by Ginsu knives.

"Your hair looks really great, Rachael."

"Thanks. Where's Lauren?"

Marshall picked up a banana and slowly peeled each side down just enough to break off a piece. He popped it into his mouth and swallowed.

"She's with one of her friends, Wendi. They're going to meet me back here, and then we'll go swimming at the Y. Want to come?"

"No, thanks. How are they getting here?"

"Who?" Marshall said.

I strove for patience. "Our daughter and her friend. Wendi?"

"Oh. Wendi's brother is driving them. He's one of my part-timers. They're just grabbing their swim suits and coming right over."

"How old is he? Let me guess. Sixteen? How long have you known him? Are you sure she'll be okay?"

"He's 18. Lighten up, Rachael."

I moved past him and out onto the porch. As promised, another vehicle, a pickup truck, was headed toward the cabin. "Hogey's dead, so you see, it's kinda hard for me to lighten up," I said, turning to Marshall.

His face grayed. "What do you mean, he's dead?"

"Just what I said. He's dead. Murdered."

At that moment the pickup truck entered the gravel drive-way, its wheels spinning so fast that when the driver slammed to a stop, gravel spewed all over the front porch. I had to bite my tongue not to yell at the redheaded kid who emerged from the driver's side.

A girl—I presumed she was Wendi—jumped out of the passenger side, followed by Lauren. The three kids bolted noisily up the steps and into the house, and I forced myself to relax. I didn't want Lauren to pick up on my bad vibes.

The redheaded boy walked up to me, blushing nervously. He glanced at Lauren, then extended his hand. Lauren's quick nod of approval wasn't lost on me. "Hello, Mrs. Grant. I'm, uh, Brandon."

"Thanks for bringing Lauren home, Brandon."

"You're, uh, welcome."

Lauren grinned and bussed my cheek. "Mom, you cut your hair! You going swimming with us?"

"No, honey. I have other plans. What happened to staying the night with Skipper?"

She rolled her eyes. "Grounded."

"Oh."

"That's okay. I can spend the night with her on Friday. She'll be free then. Who did your hair?" Lauren flipped her fingers through my hair. "It really looks great. I gotta get my bathing suit. Know where it is?"

I glanced at Brandon, noting his adoring gaze as he watched Lauren. He glanced at me. I raised one eyebrow and tried to look stern. He blushed again and looked away. To Lauren I said, "Jamie cut it. Ever think of trying your dresser drawers?"

She rolled her eyes. "Mom," she said, somehow making the word into three syllables. She and Wendi ran into her room. Brandon sat on the edge of the couch, his hands clenching and unclenching nervously.

"Rachael," Marshall whispered, glancing toward Brandon. "What about Hogey?"

I motioned for him to follow me back out onto the front porch. Once the door was closed behind us, I said, "I went to Granddad's house, and Hogey was inside. In Granddad's room."

"Was he. . . ."

I ran my hands through my hair. It felt strange. It would take me a while to get used to it. "Just like Stanley, only he wasn't hanging from the rafters."

Marshall's face paled beneath his windburn. "I think you should go home, Rachael."

I shook my head. "I can't. Now, especially." I didn't want to go into all my reasons, but if Fernando was behind this, it didn't matter where I was. He'd find me. For some reason I felt safer here in Saddle Gap, despite having two corpses practically at my feet.

But there was one thing I could do. "Marshall, I want Lauren to stay with you for a couple of days." He looked taken aback and shook his head. I frowned, not expecting that reaction.

"Maybe she could stay with your granddad when he gets back?"

I grimaced. "Granddad might not even get to stay in his own home for a while."

"Well." He sighed and glanced at the police cruiser. "I guess that would be okay. I've been staying at Mom's. To help out, I mean." His face flushed. "Lauren can stay in the guest room. How long are you planning on staying, anyway?" he finished in a rush.

"I'm not sure."

Marshall glanced at his watch. "Well, what are you going to do about school? Spring break is almost over, you know."

"I know. I'm not sure what I'm going to do."

"Why not enroll her here?"

I looked at him in surprise. "Here? Marshall, isn't that going a bit far? I can call her school on Monday. Explain the situation. They can send her work here. It can't last much longer. I hope."

"I don't know, Rachael. Maybe you'll be here longer than you think." The corner of his mouth lifted, and he nodded toward the front door. "I think Lauren'd like to stay and finish out the year, too."

"Marshall, he's 18!" I hissed.

He grinned.

The last thing I wanted was for my daughter to repeat her mother's mistake. I'd been 13, Marshall 18, when we first met. I did not want my daughter with a toddler before she was 20. No way. I reached for the door handle.

"Besides," Marshall said, "maybe it'd be best for you, too."

I stopped, my hand on the door. "Why do you say that?"

He shrugged. "I heard your leg wasn't doing so hot."

A burning started in the pit of my stomach, gnawing gleefully away. "Who told you that?"

He dropped his head.

"Come on, Marshall." I had to know what he'd heard.

He sighed, rubbing his hands roughly over his face. He dropped his hands, then looked out toward the waiting police car, not looking at me. "Brandon's mom works at Malik Goodnight's clinic. She overheard him talking on the phone to someone."

"So she immediately called you up and blabbed a private conversation?"

"She knew I was worried about you, Rachael," he said. A sad, hesitant look crossed his face. "I care about what happens to you. I know how much your work means to you. That's all."

I immediately deflated. Leaning against the doorjamb, I looked out across the road in front of the river house, into the field beyond. Indian paintbrush, purple sage, and wild thyme blew in rhythmic waves, bowing to the wind's command. It was so quiet out here. Peaceful. In direct contrast to the feelings boiling inside of me. "What else did she say, Marshall."

"That it didn't look good. That being shot through, like you were, the muscle damage might never repair itself."

The flowers across the road blurred, and a lump so big it felt like a boulder lodged in my throat. "Damn," I whispered. Why hadn't my doctor said anything? Why hadn't Malik said something?

Or maybe they had. Maybe I just wasn't listening.

"What are you going to do?" Marshall asked.

"I really don't know." Inside the house, the three teenagers' voices rose in laughter. "I think you'd better go toss them into the pool. Cool off those raging hormones before they set my cabin on fire." I pushed open the door.

Marshall nodded, then caught me in his arm. He leaned over and kissed me on the cheek. "I'm sorry, Rachael," he whispered into my ear, "Just be careful, okay? I mean that. As a friend."

"Thanks. That means a lot, Marshall." On impulse, I gave him a quick hug.

Unfortunately, Lauren walked out just then. Her eyes

widened and her mouth dropped open. Her face flushed as she grinned in pleasure.

The realization hit me. Did she believe her mom and dad would get back together? Did she see him kiss me? A kiss meant only one thing to a 13 year old.

I groaned and headed for the bedroom, leaving Marshall to round up Lauren's things. It looked like my daughter and I would have to have a long talk. Real soon.

No sooner had I sent Lauren off with her father and her friends than a dusty white Volvo appeared at the end of the road. A smile erupted from deep within me, banishing, at least temporarily, the storm that had been gathering in my mind.

Jenn had arrived.

I waited as she parked. I waited some more as she extricated herself from the front seat. It was my inclination to run down and help her, even in my current state, but I'd learned long ago that when she needed or wanted help, she'd let me know.

"I'm coming, Rachael. Don't you fret," she hollered.

"Well, hurry it on up, girlfriend. Else I'll fall asleep waiting on you."

"Wench."

She pulled two silver canes from the passenger side. I knew she was up to no good when she paused and shrugged a bulky backpack onto her back. *Uh-oh.* When she finally hauled herself to her feet and started to make her way to the house, I opened the front door.

Though Jenn didn't mind my watching her slow, painful progress, I knew she preferred not to have an audience. I'd moved into the kitchen by the time she made it to the front door.

"Whew, Rachael. Why couldn't you have insisted on an elevator?"

I smiled and, balancing on my crutch, accepted the backpack Jenn handed to me. "Mac probably would install one if I asked him."

She chuckled. "Don't need an elevator if you've a fresh

batch of my Rock-em Zonk-em Salsa. One bite and I guarantee it'll rocket you to the rooftop. Landing gear not included."

"I'd rather stay safe on the ground for now. How is Elton these days?"

She smiled a very self-satisfied smile. "Good, good, good. Very good."

I laughed. "That good, huh?"

"Oh, yes, honey. That good."

Elton and Jenn's love affair was legendary in these parts. They'd met on the rodeo circuit fifteen years before. Elton is a rodeo doctor who travels all over the state. Jenn used to accompany him, along with their young son, until about six years ago, when a freight trailer, pulled by a truck ahead of them, had somehow unhitched itself. Jenn, who'd been driving, ran straight into it. She'd nearly died. She claims she lived only because of Elton—and their son.

And, she admitted once to me, because of her chili peppers. Jenn had been in the midst of creating a surefire winner for the Texas Chili Cook-Off that season when the accident happened. She won that year, too, though it took Elton, her son, and a private nurse to help her do it.

Now she owned a salsa and chili supply company and tamale bar that folks traveled hundreds of miles to visit. Though we'd been friends in school, we'd lost touch. I'd remet her several years before, when I was visiting and Granddad asked me to run into town to buy a batch of stuffed jalapeños.

I loved Jenn's stuffed jalapeños. I admired the jar of fresh salsa she'd brought, and, unable to resist, I opened the jar. Cilantro, tomato, and the sharp tang of something else I didn't recognize wafted into the kitchen. I rolled my eyes and sighed in ecstasy. "Heaven. Sheer heaven."

"There's some blue tortilla chips in there, too. And some chili mix. Elton's latest attempt."

I looked at my friend skeptically and asked, "He using me as a guinea pig?"

She chuckled but looked at the ceiling.

"Thought so. You want some coffee?"

"Sure." She slapped her hand down. "So, what's going on here, Rachael?"

While I filled the carafe in the sink, I filled Jenn in on everything I knew about my grandfather's decision to sell Tumbleweeds to Stanley Fletcher, and what little I knew about Stanley's death. I also told her about Hogey. And about Fernando and his threats to hurt me and my daughter.

The coffee finished brewing, and, one at a time, I took our mugs to the table. Jenn moved over to the easy chair.

"We're quite the pair, aren't we?" she said.

I smiled as I arranged myself on the couch. "I never realized crutches were such a pain."

"Hands hurt? There's this stuff—"

"I know, Marshall told me. For cow udders."

Jenn gave me a perplexed look. "Cow udders. Girlfriend, you have been in the city too long. It's some lotion I buy at the pharmacy. Good stuff."

"Oh."

She grinned. "Just teasing. Udder Butter works miracles. Get some."

"Marshall's bringing me some—or so he promised."

"He still putting the pressure on you?"

I contemplated Jenn's question for a moment, then slowly shook my head. "Actually, no. He's been a regular Joe since I've been back this time."

"That's a switch."

"Yeah, but it's put ideas into Lauren's head." *And Jamie's,* I thought, remembering the swimsuit. "We're not getting along that way. Just as friends."

"Nice."

I nodded. "Yeah, it is, actually."

Jenn took a sip of her coffee. "Now, let's talk about this Fernando guy. Do you really think he could pose a threat to you here?"

I yawned and settled myself down further into the couch. The steam wafted from my coffee mug, and I breathed in, grateful for its warmth. The aroma comforted me, as did the companionship of my friend.

"I don't know, Jenn. Fernando's hate for me is pretty strong. I think he may be as obsessed about killing me as I am about capturing him. But whether or not— Hold on." I got up again and went into the kitchen. The package Dave sent me waited patiently, leaning against the toaster. I tucked it beneath my arm and returned to the couch.

"What's that?"

"My mail from home." I opened the package and slid the contents out. "Phone bill, gas bill, electric bill, several more bills, how lovely. Letter from a friend in Georgia, a hospital bill. Lordy, I don't want to look at that."

"Anything good?"

"No. I asked Dave to check my mail just in case Fernando tracked me down there, but it doesn't look like there's anything. He's been sending threatening letters to me at work, but not to the house. He even sent me a dozen roses."

"Roses? What on earth for? Maybe he was trying to make amends."

I grimaced. "Ha. They were dead roses."

Jenn shuddered. "Does he know where you live? Here, I mean."

"No. At least I don't think so. So I doubt he had anything to do with Stanley. Or Hogey." I bit my thumbnail, then shook my head. "That's not the right track."

Jenn shook her head. "I hope not. But I worry about you, you know. I don't like to admit it, but frankly, I wish you'd leave that line of work behind."

"It's all I know, Jenn."

"Shoot. You learned how to be a cop. You can learn to do something else. What about the ranch?"

I shook my head. "We won't find out what the status of that is until tomorrow, if then." I thumped the sofa. Frustration made me want to tear out what little hair I had left. "I've got to find who did this, Jenn. The bastard. I can't believe someone would kill Hogey! Why? Stanley wasn't liked too much, but did he deserve to die? No. Of course not. Somewhere, there's got to be a connection. There's got to be. I've got to figure out what it is, or I'll go nuts."

I took a deep breath, dropped my head in my hands, and rolled it back and forth, my eyes squeezed shut. All I could see was Hogey—dear, drunk, innocent Hogey—sprawled across the chair. Why him? What did he know? What connection did he have with Stanley?

I raised my head and grabbed my cup of coffee and, ignoring its temperature, downed it in a few swallows. "I've got to figure this out, Jenn. I've got to. For Granddad's sake. For everyone who works at Tumbleweeds. What's going to happen to them now? To Cathy?"

I shook my head, briefly overwhelmed by the responsibility on my shoulders. "Do you know what?" I said. "After I saw Hogey, dead like that, I actually threw up. Me, cast-iron-stomach Rachael, throwing up." I brushed my hand across my face, angry at my eyes for suddenly tearing up. "I couldn't handle it."

Jenn put down her cup. She leaned forward, as earnest as I'd ever seen her. "Listen to me, Rachael. Do you remember what you told me, oh, a couple of years ago, when I came to visit?"

I frowned, trying to remember. I shook my head. "I don't. No. What did I say?"

"It was after we went to that bar."

"Oh. Well, I barely remember anything past that bar," I said, feeling sheepish. "What did I say?"

"You told me this, Rachael Grant. You said, 'If I ever change, if I ever become hard, bitter, indifferent to what I'm doing, Jenn, tell me to stop. Tell me I have to quit. I don't want to be like that. I don't want to forget what it's like to care.'"

I shifted uncomfortably on the couch. "I don't remember saying that," I said evasively.

She leaned over and patted my hand and smiled, a gentle, knowing smile. "I think you do, Rachael, honey."

"But I'm not like that." My conversation with Nick at Granddad's house rang in my mind. "Not now."

"You were well on your way to it, then. You just couldn't see it."

I stared down at my coffee and slowly nodded my head.

"Nothing else mattered except getting through the next day, collaring the next bad guy. That was all you used to talk about."

"I had to be that way. To survive. We all did."

"We all *did*," Jenn repeated. "Past tense. I think there's a part of you that has already left that life of yours behind, Rachael. I don't think you want to go back to being a cop."

I wanted to cover my ears. I didn't want to hear this. Not from Jenn, too. "I'm good at what I do."

"I know you are, honey. But is it really worth it? You've been shot, and now this man wants you dead. They'll pick him up eventually, put him in jail, but for how long, Rachael? For how long?"

She had me there. "Never long enough."

"In the next fifteen years, how many more Fernandos will you encounter? Maybe it's time to turn the job over to someone else. Let someone else accumulate the Fernandos. I think you've been wanting to, anyway. You didn't want me or anyone else to tell you, but you've been thinking about it. Haven't you?"

"You know, it's a good thing I love you so much," I said.

Jenn smiled. "Haven't you?" she repeated.

"Maybe. A little."

"Maybe it's time to think about other areas of your life. Like the ranch. Like your daughter. Like Nick."

I sucked in my breath. "What about Nick?"

"I know my little brother. Very well. It's taken him a while, but I figured he'd get around to courting you soon enough."

"Courting me? You must be kidding."

She chuckled. "He's been in love with you since we were teenagers."

"Why didn't I know this?"

She cocked her head toward me. "You're a hard lady to catch standing still, but he's a patient man."

"This is your brother we're talking about, Jenn. I don't need anyone in my life right now."

"Then why are you blushing?"

"Latent effects of overexertion."

"Bull." Jenn's expression grew serious. "He's a great guy, Rachael. He'd make one heck of a great lover."

Now I was blushing. "You can't talk about your own brother that way."

"Why not? I love him. I love you. You two together would

— 111 —

make me very happy."

"But I won't be here."

"So you say."

"Besides," I said, waving my hand in dismissal of her calm assurance as to my future, "he's leaving for Border Patrol Academy in just a few days."

She smiled. "So what? Let me tell you, honey. Long-distance loving can be the best kind. Ask Elton."

I laughed, but Jenn's speech had left me shaken. She knew me too well, probably better than I knew myself. I wasn't ready to settle down with anyone, much less give up my work. No way. For ten years, work had been everything to me. Even all my friends were cops. They were my family. How could I give all that up?

I couldn't, I thought. At least, not yet. I shifted on the couch as a particularly vicious stab of pain shot through my leg, making me wonder if I really had a choice.

Chapter 11

THE SOUND OF RAIN striking my bedroom window woke me the next morning, far earlier than I wanted to wake up. I glanced at the clock—it was already nine? I hadn't slept until nine since, well, I couldn't even remember since when.

Jenn had stayed late into the evening, until Elton phoned and commanded she come home. After promising to keep her ears peeled for anything that might help us figure out what happened to Stanley, she finally left and I collapsed into bed.

Smushing myself down into the covers, I fought to get over the guilty feeling of laziness. I closed my eyes, determined to go back to sleep, but my brain, once awake, refused to shut down.

The previous day's events slammed back into my mind. I slammed them out again, burrowing myself into my pillow, yanking the covers up to my chin. Hogey's laughing face toyed with my conscience, forcing my eyes open as the laughter was replaced by a silent scream.

Damn. I flopped onto my back and stared at the ceiling fan as it turned in lazy circles. I had to decide what to do.

I'm a cop, I reminded myself. Trained to deal with situations that arise on a daily basis on the streets. Assault. Rape. Theft. Chasing the bad guy, capturing him, and then, like a well-trained cop should, handing him over for others to deal with.

Until my encounter with Flash Fernando, I'd always done what was expected. Gone by the book. Hung up my emotions and jumped back out onto the streets. I grimaced. Just like Jenn had accused.

But I couldn't let Fernando go, and I couldn't let Stanley's and Hogey's murders go, either. Jenn was right about that. I should be content to pass the investigative role over to those trained to handle such matters—and leave it at that—but it wasn't going to happen, no matter what Marshall, Boone, Granddad, Nick, or even Lauren thought.

I wasn't ready to give up. At least, not yet.

Two people were dead, both killed brutally. Neither one of the victims was the kind of person to be considered a threat. Hogey was so harmless it was almost pathetic.

Who were we dealing with here? Why Stanley, and why Hogey? And what could I do about it?

The warning from Boone was quite clear, so I'd have to strike out on my own. I needed to make a list.

Grabbing a pen and paper from my bedside table, I sat up and used my good leg as a prop. At the top of the list I wrote, "Interview the Conard brothers." They were Hogey's running buddies and probably the last to see him alive.

I also needed to talk to Cathy. I wrote her name down and underlined it and went on, not wanting to dwell on Hogey's wife too long. What was she going to do now with two babies to feed? She hadn't worked outside the home in years. Though Hogey was a bit of a lush and not the smartest man I'd ever known, he had always been faithful to his work at the ranch. He loved his horses. If I stayed in Saddle Gap and somehow got Tumbleweeds back, I could help Cathy and her sons, I thought.

I paused for a moment and listened to the rain outside. Without thinking, I reached to the empty space beside me, my hand resting on nothing but air. I sighed. Boy, did I miss my dog.

"Send for Higgins," I noted on the pad. I didn't want to consider what it would cost to ship an 80-pound fur ball from San Antonio to Saddle Gap. The thought of all that thick, long fur tangling in sandburs set my teeth on edge.

Back to the list. I wrote down "Tumbleweeds," underlined it twice, and started a list underneath that. How long had Stanley lurked around there, trying to make up his mind about buying the place? Had he and Hogey ever crossed paths? Did they have mutual friends? Where did Stanley live?

Next, I wrote down "Lacey Halloran." Did her sister Bethy have anything to do with all this, or was Lacey just a poor, angry woman who was right to be glad Stanley was out of the picture?

I found myself writing down another name: "Nick." I immediately scratched it out.

Nuts. I had more important things to worry about than my love life. I couldn't drag him into this, either. I needed to handle this underhanded investigation on my own—soon enough, I might have to rely on Nick for legitimate help.

First, though, I'd need to get wheels. I moved my leg slightly, wincing at the pain. A Volkswagen would be out of the question, but maybe I could manage with a nice used Honda. I smiled. Even that would be a treat after years of dealing with the cantankerous Cloud.

Rolling onto my side, I shoved a pillow under my aching leg and stared out the window. Outside was a blur of rain-streaked green. Here in Saddle Gap, we didn't get as much rain as some folks did, and I knew that whatever moisture had been granted the small town would be sucked into the water-starved soil within an hour or so.

As if it knew what I was thinking about, the rain patter increased, striking against the window with enthusiasm. Now that I'd made a decision to act, I felt oddly relaxed and enjoyed listening to the rain. The only other sounds in the house were the hum of the refrigerator, the ticking of the mantel clock, and the muffled sound of the television.

I bolted upright. Television? Grabbing my robe, I fought to ignore my stiff muscles as I wrestled it on. I reached for my gun.

Then the just-ripped-open smell of fresh coffee wafted into the room. I snapped my head up. Coffee . . . and what else? Cinnamon rolls? Hobbling to the edge of my doorway, I poked my head cautiously around the corner.

A small, plump woman dressed in a bright red Mexican dress sat primly on the couch, her sparkling black eyes fixed on a Jerry Springer wrestling match. Raven-black hair, liberally sprinkled with gray, was pulled back from her face into a neat bun at the back of her neck.

Her exclamations of "Oh!" and "Oh, my!" were the only clues to her level of enthusiasm for the show. Her small but capable hands lay firmly clasped in her lap, her plump feet encased in shiny new black leather pumps crossed neatly at the ankles. Neat as a pin and sharp as always. I don't believe I've ever seen Carmita in any sort of disarray, even when elbow deep in cooking for ten employees and twice as many guests.

I leaned against the doorjamb and cleared my throat. Her head whipped around, her eyes widening in surprise. "Rachael!"

I smiled and took a deep, happy breath. "Carmita. You're home." I laid my gun on top of the dresser, then went into the room. She rose gracefully and waited, her arms outstretched. I let myself be folded into her warm embrace.

"Rachael, sweetheart. I'm sorry I woke you."

"That's okay. Congratulations," I murmured as I hugged her tight.

"Thank you, Rachael." She pulled away from me and looked up into my face, her dark eyes darting back and forth. "Are you sure? Your granddad said you took the news well."

I hesitated, but only for the briefest of moments. "Of course I'm sure. How long—" I stopped, feeling not a little nosy. "I'm sorry. That's none of my business."

She helped me settle onto the couch, grabbing a blanket and tucking it around me. "Of course it is." A soft smile played across her face. She looked over my shoulder and said, "I've loved him from the first, Rachael. It just took the salty old cur a decade to realize it."

"Hey, now, woman," Granddad said. "If'n you'd ever speak up any, I'da known beforehand."

I twisted around. "Granddad! Come sit down. What are you doing back so soon?" I watched as he enthusiastically trotted over to the couch opposite mine. *No broken legs on the slopes*, I breathed thankfully. Carmita eased into the kitchen, and before Granddad could answer, I had a hot cinnamon roll on a plate shoved into one hand, a steaming cup of coffee in the other.

Granddad's face fell. "We got a phone call yesterday, about Hogey."

Oh. "I'm sorry, Granddad. I should have called you—"

He held his hand up. "Don't worry about it. Sheriff Rosa took care of it." His gaze flicked to Carmita. "He said it'd be best if we come on back."

Carmita settled down next to Granddad. I had to smile. They really did look quite good together, now that they'd given themselves permission to acknowledge their mutual affection. He, the sun-weathered, rough-and-tumble cowboy; she, the ever-proper lady.

"How'd you get in here, anyway?"

"Mac left a set of keys for me. We ran by the house, but it looks like we'll be staying at a motel for a day or two. Right, Carmita?"

She gazed adoringly at her new husband, and he patted her knee. It was hard now to believe I'd ever questioned Carmita's loyalty to him.

"I'm glad you're back. Maybe now we can get some answers. Granddad, what is the status of Tumbleweeds?"

Carmita and Granddad looked at each other for a long moment, then turned to me in unison.

"Well," Granddad began, "best the sheriff's been able to figure out, Stanley had no kin. The money was all transferred to me, so's that's not to worry about. It was a legal deal, Rachael, honey. But. . . ."

I took a bite of my cinnamon roll and closed my eyes. Heaven. "So. . . ," I prompted.

He shifted uncomfortably on the couch.

"Go on, dear," Carmita encouraged him as I set down my cinnamon roll and picked up the cup of coffee.

"Put that thing down a second, Rachael," Granddad said.

"What?" I put the mug down.

His shoulders slumped a little, and he grasped Carmita's hand.

"Just say it quick, Arthur," she encouraged.

He cleared his throat. "Well, seems that the sheriff wants you to come around to his office today, about noon."

"I was going there anyway. I need to sign my statement. . . ."

My words died off as the look was exchanged again. "Grand-dad. What's going on here?"

"Well, seems like Stanley left the ranch in capable hands."

"Whose? I thought you said he had no kin."

"That's right. He didn't leave it to no kin, Rachael. Seems Stanley left the ranch to you."

I was at the sheriff's department a few minutes early, despite having to drive left-footed, my injured leg thrown onto the passenger side.

Carmita's car was small, but as neat as the woman who owned it. She'd brooked no argument over handing me the keys; I was not to waste my money on a rental. Visions of driving a luxury liner flew out the window in the face of such opposition. But she did have a CD of Jennifer Lopez. There was obviously a lot I still needed to learn about Carmita.

Whipping the car into a parking space, I turned it off, cutting J.Lo short. I eased out the door, grabbed my crutch, and locked the car.

The surprise morning rain had tapered off, leaving short-lived puddles in my path. The sky overhead remained overcast, threatening more precipitation, but most of the cars in the parking lot had open windows. A quick glance at the vehicles assured me Nick's car wasn't among the police cruisers. I went inside.

The sheriff's office was busy for lunchtime. Various deputies milled about, some carrying clipboards, others carrying on conversations. One or two glanced my way, brief flashes of recognition followed by solemn dips of the head. I nodded back to those who felt obliged to acknowledge me.

A twenty-something young woman, with a phone glued to her ear and dressed in jeans and a Mickey Mouse T-shirt, sat at the front counter. I waited for her to finish her conversation, taking advantage of the moment to glance around the room.

Behind the receptionist were several desks, all empty. Each one was decorated suitably to the taste of the unseen occupant—one covered with frogs, another with teddy bears. Cute. Sheriff Rosa's office was at the back of the corral of secretaries and clerks. His door was closed.

Conversation ebbed and flowed behind me as different personnel moved in and out. Each time a door opened, I found myself starting. Nick wasn't the only person I didn't want to run into.

Unfortunately, a voice that could belong only to Investigator Boone carried through the office at that very moment. Damn. I wanted to talk with Sheriff Rosa, see how he felt now that this investigation had been snapped from his pudgy clutches. I had to move fast.

The receptionist froze, her mouth a round O of surprise, as she looked toward the sound of Boone's booming voice. The poor girl's eyes clearly betrayed her horror. Without saying goodbye, she slammed the phone down. Ah, an ally.

"I'm Rachael Grant."

The receptionist's head swiveled back and forth between me and the door where Boone would walk through any second. "Oh! Ms. Grant, the sheriff—"

"Is he in his office?"

"I don't—"

I shoved through the gate. "Good, I'll just go see him now."

She squealed. "You can't go in there! I mean, I gotta announce you—"

My hand was on the sheriff's door. I looked over my shoulder. Deputies scurried into the room in front of Boone like so many brown sparrows being chased by a cat. "Then I suggest you make that call. Or leave and pretend you didn't see me."

The receptionist grinned in relief. "I'm out of here." She grabbed her purse and ran from her desk.

I dove into Sheriff Rosa's office and shut the door behind me. I had to fight not to slam it.

"Rachael! What in the blazes—"

I pointed my thumb back over my shoulder. "Sorry, Sheriff Rosa. I didn't want to talk to Investigator Boone before I had a chance to speak with you. Your receptionist wasn't there."

He stared at me for a long moment with a hang-dog expression, then shook his head, which sent his jowls waggling. I had to wonder how much beer and barbecue the man consumed. "All righty, Rachael. Hold on a sec."

He picked up the phone and spoke urgently into it. When he placed the receiver back on the cradle, he positively beamed.

"Now, Rachael. I'm glad you came by here. Sit down, sit down." He clapped his hands together. "Want some coffee?"

"No, thanks. Sheriff Rosa, I hope you don't mind my just coming on over, barging in like this."

"No problem. You talked to your granddaddy?"

I nodded. "Yes, sir. And that's what I don't understand. He said Stanley left the guest ranch to me? I find that hard to believe."

I watched Rosa's dappled face ripple in consternation, his eyes blinking rapidly as he weighed what to do. Through the door we could hear Boone's voice booming. I think that did the trick. Something told me Sheriff Rosa and Boone didn't get along too well.

"That's right, Rachael. Left the whole dang thing to you."

I scooted to the edge of my seat. "He had a will?"

"Yes, ma'am, he sure did. Now, I don't have a copy of it right with me," he said. "But I saw it. It's all legal."

I figured, of course, Boone had the will. "Where was it drawn?"

"Drawn? Oh, you mean where did he get it all signed and all. Law firm by the name of Norton & Dorland, over in Marfa. They'll be wanting you to come see them as soon as you can." He handed me a card. It was from Bunny's, a local bar. A name and phone number were scratched on the back in what I presumed was the sheriff's handwriting. "This here's the name of the fellow I talked to. He said you could come by tomorrow afternoon."

"That's fine. Stanley had no family? No one special to leave it to?"

"No, sure didn't, sounds like."

I decided to take a stab at seeing what I could get from him. "Sheriff, how exactly did Stanley really die?"

His face lit up again. Jackpot. He leaned close to me, so close I could see every pockmark on his face, every red vein in his eyes. The sheriff had lost some sleep on this one. "Morphine."

I sat back. "Morphine? Morphine's relatively easy to get."

"Not as easy as you might think."

"What other leads are there?"

His face fell into a scowl. "Well, Rachael, you'll have to ask Investigator Boone that question."

"She's not keeping you informed?" I said, surprised.

"Hell, no." He leaned forward, his hands clenched. "Just between you and me, Rachael, that woman makes me angrier'n a skunk in a rainstorm." He shot back in his chair and thumped his feet up on the desk. "Damn Yankee."

I had to smother a smile. "But I thought you were working on this case together."

"Nope. She's using my office and staff and all, but, far's I know, there's nothing else." He leaned toward me. "Morphine was found in Stanley's system. Loads of it. Someone got it into him somehow or other. When we—excuse me—when Investigator Boone finds out who, why, there's our murderer."

"And I suppose you yourself have some *who*'s in mind? Even though you aren't really participating in this investigation?"

He shot me a look. "You know something, Rachael, I knew your daddy. He was the stubbornest boy I ever encountered, and watching you grow up, well, as they say, the blossom didn't fall far from the peach tree. Always did admire that about you."

Sheriff Rosa surprised me. I had no idea he knew my father, though I suppose Rosa was in his early fifties, about the age my dad would have been if he hadn't died. My dad always taught me to go for the truth and, if I wanted something, to go get it.

"Thanks. I guess."

"It's a good trait to have, especially when one suspects that the who did it in a whodunit is the wrong person."

Now I was perplexed. "Are you trying to say you think Boone is focusing on the wrong person?"

"I'm not saying that at all. I just think she don't have all the answers, and she has it in her head I don't either. My hands are tied, Rachael, and as I've said, I don't like it."

"I don't like being kept in the dark, either. I don't even know the things I should know out of common courtesy, as Hogey's family. That's all I'm really trying to find out."

He considered me for a long moment, then slowly shook his head. "Boone's already told you that she won't tolerate you snooping around. But what she really gonna do to you?"

I shrugged and smiled. "Nothing, really."

"That's right. Nothing." He paused again. "There's nothing I can do to help you directly," he said, emphasizing the last word.

He pulled open a desk drawer, then pulled out a folder and laid it on his desk. "You know something, Rachael? It's a real pain in the keister to have to share this office." He thumped the folder. "Folks leave all kinds of stuff sitting about."

He lumbered to his feet but held up a hand as I started to rise. "No, no, you stay here. I'll send a deputy to bring your statement in so's you can sign it." He tipped his hat to me. "Be careful now. You hear? I'm going fishing. Get away from this mess for a while."

Then he was gone.

I stared at the folder for a long moment. Then I remembered—Granddad had said Sheriff Rosa had specifically asked to see me at lunchtime, when the office all but shut down, even though he knew I was coming in to sign my statement. I shook my head. Sheriff Rosa was, indeed, an unusual sheriff.

I opened the folder. Inside was a thin stack of papers. Copies, it looked like, made on a very old copy machine. I sifted through them—autopsy notes which verified the morphine overdose, witness statements from the Conard brothers, a list of names.

There were a few photographs of different people, including me. One stopped me short. It was the Glory Wall picture of me, Pamela, Jamie, her face beaming with pride, and Marshall, holding a deer. Someone must have picked it up from Tumbleweeds. But something bothered me.

I needed to know if this photograph was the same as the one I'd left back on Granddad's desk. I would swear on my parents' graves that nothing had been written on the back, but this had "got him" on the back in neat, squared-off letters. All caps. How had Boone obtained this? From whom? As far as I knew, no copies were ever made of the pictures Granddad took for the Glory Wall.

I set the photographs aside and scanned the list of names. Beside Pamela's name was written "nurse" in parentheses. Easy enough for a nurse to get morphine. But why in the world would Pamela care who owned Tumbleweeds? That explained the question mark beside her name. No known motive. Except, maybe, revenge? Her father had been ruined by Stanley, after all. Pamela's strange behavior in the grocery store came back to me, too. I scratched the thought about no known motive. Pamela had every reason to hate Stanley and want to see him dead. But the timing was strange. Why wait all these years to kill him?

Hogey's name was second. No reason for him to kill Stanley that I could see. Besides, now he was dead, too. There were two question marks by his name.

My name was next. And beside my name was written "revenge?" "disgruntled over sale?" and "inherited ranch."

Marshall's name followed. The words "bankruptcy" and "blackmail" were beside his name, along with "inheritance" and "bow hunting."

A strange heat flushed my face. Chills ran down my back. Did Boone suspect Marshall? Just because one time, and only one time, he shot a deer with a bow and arrow? No way. And what about the bankruptcy? And blackmail? I had a feeling it was time to have a serious talk with my ex. Not that he owed me explanations or anything, unless what he'd kept from me was responsible in some part for Hogey's and Stanley's deaths.

The rest of the list consisted of folks like Cathy, Jamie, Carmita, Granddad, a few names I didn't recognize, and others I remembered from my welcome-home party. I'd have to look into the ones that didn't sound familiar. The party had been attended by several people I didn't know, but I had just assumed they were guests at the ranch. Maybe not.

Voices filtered through the door. I hurriedly took everything but the photographs from the folder and tucked the copies beneath my arm. I grabbed my crutch and opened the door, relieved to see only a clerk or two coming back from lunch. I moved quickly through the office and breathed a sigh of relief when I made it safely to my car.

Then I stopped. The statement. Oh, well, they would have to wait. I had some unofficial sleuthing to do.

Chapter 12

WHILE I WAS INSIDE the sheriff's office, the temperature outside had risen a good twenty degrees. All traces of moisture were gone, sucked up and evaporated. It was 1:00, and suddenly I had too much to do and not enough time to do it. Some of the errands would have to be put off until the next day.

I had an appointment tomorrow at Stanley's lawyer's office in Marfa. They had absolutely no explanation as to why Stanley had chosen me as his heir. He had no others, had been adamant I be named. The whole thing was weird, but legitimate.

I needed to talk to Dave, too. And Granddad, about Tumbleweeds. The workers had been given a week off, that much I knew. I'd have to drive out there and see what, if anything, was going on, and sift through the office again.

I also needed to visit Hogey's widow. I didn't look forward to this at all, and knew I couldn't do it on an empty stomach. A quick stop at the Czech Shoppe was definitely in order. And there was a friend I wanted to see. I headed downtown to the Courthouse Square.

A few minutes later I pulled Carmita's car into a parking space in front of Marshall's John Deere store and got out. I locked the car door, realized I'd locked my crutch inside, unlocked the door again, and got my crutch out. After a few awkward moments I hobbled into Marshall's store.

As expected, bright, excited faces gleamed at me the moment I stepped inside the main showroom. One of the slick-suited salesmen slithered from behind one of the shiny new tractors. "May I help you?"

I glanced around. I seldom intruded on him here. "Is Marshall here?"

The man frowned. "Marshall, Marshall, oh. No. I'm sorry, but he's not here."

He usually took vacation when Lauren was in town. "All right, thanks. I'll catch him later."

The slick smile returned. "Would you like one of our brochures?"

"No, thanks. I'm not in the market for a tractor." I grabbed the door handle and escaped just as the gleam brightened in the salesman's eye.

I had to close my own eyes for a second as I stood outside the store, the sun was shining with such intensity. But though the temperature was rising steadily, that hadn't kept any of the locals or even the tourists away from Saddle Gap. Downtown bustled with energy. A small group of gray-haired women wearing bright Mexican dresses, accompanied by stooped men in Bermuda shorts with desert hats perched jauntily on their balding heads, haggled good-naturedly with one of the Mexican fruit-stand vendors.

"No, no. I won't pay three dollars for this." The woman held up the odd star-shaped piece of fruit and eyed it suspiciously. "I don't even know what it is. Are you sure it's good?"

"Si. Four dollars." The vendor beamed. He leaned back on his heels and grinned.

"Well, I don't know. Marcus? What is this thing?"

One of the elderly men broke off from the group and shuffled over to his wife. He peered through the bottom of his bifocals. "Well, Rachael, I don't know quite what that thing is."

Rachael? I grinned, catching the vendor's eye.

He winked. "One dollar. Si? Yes?" He reached out to the woman but didn't touch her. "For you, dear Rachael. My favorite name, it is Rachael. Rachael means sweet lamb of God. Did you know that?" The woman blushed. "All Rachaels I know are sweet. And beautiful as newborn lambs. Si?"

I laughed. The other Rachael glanced over her shoulder at me and grinned.

"It's really good," I said. "From one Rachael to another."

The woman's face brightened and she looked at the vendor. "Oh! Well, then. If you say so. I'll take it."

I waited patiently as she fished in her purse and handed

Gilbert a dollar. He deftly wrapped the star fruit, put it into a bag, bowed his head, and handed it to the woman. With a chuckle she took the bag, and she and her husband rejoined their friends.

Once they were out of earshot, I admonished Gil. "Four dollars?"

He looked aghast. "No! Not four dollars. Three, if I'm lucky. But I will take one. What do you think I am? A thief?"

I grinned.

"No. Don't answer that."

"Wise man," I said with a chuckle.

Gilbert and I had met in San Antonio. For three years he'd been a thorn in my side. I'd hauled him in at least once a month for petty theft. Finally, he was sentenced to community service and became a street vendor, choosing at last to go legit. Though I didn't condone his original method for making money, I did applaud his reasons, which were the same as too many other regulars I knew—to send money to his very poor family in Mexico.

From our first meeting, I'd taken a crazy liking to the short, jovial, but intensely passionate man. The love he had for his wife and children was unmatched. He was a breath of fresh air compared to the Fernandos in the world. Once he'd served his time and paid his fines, he'd come to Saddle Gap. I'd helped him get started here, though he and I were the only ones who knew it. Even his wife didn't know.

Now I was the one who needed help. "Can we talk? Do you have time for a cup of coffee at the Czech Shoppe?"

He nodded. "Si. For you, anything." Waving to his oldest son to take over, Gil wiped his hands and joined me. As we walked toward the restaurant, Gil filled me in on his family. His eldest son had joined him at the fruit stand after school in the afternoons and was on the high school football team. "Place kicker. My boy, he send that ball flying!"

I laughed. "How about the other kids?"

He grinned, waving at some of the passersby. In fact, as we crossed the street and ambled up the other side of the square, Gil must have greeted a dozen or more people.

"The children, they are doing fine. Good grades and many

friends. Life is so rich here, Rachael." He paused, laying one hand on my arm. "It is sad, though, isn't it?" He waved his hand to the horizon, which hid the border between Saddle Gap and Mexico. "Such happiness here, such sadness there. And so close. Were it not for you. . . ." He raised his hands. "For you, anything. What do you need, Rachael? Why did you seek out this old thief?"

"I'll tell you. Let's eat." We entered the restaurant and sat at a table in the corner. After ordering, I asked him if he'd heard about Stanley and Hogey.

He nodded sagely, running his hand over his chin. "Si. I heard. I knew this Stanley character." He frowned in distaste. "No one liked him much."

"Like who?"

"Did you know he tried to buy more than your granddad's ranch?"

I shook my head. "No. But I don't think he had any other properties in his possession." At least not that I knew of. I'd find out tomorrow for sure.

"No one would sell their shops to him. He was a weasel."

"Have you seen anything else? Heard anything that could possibly link Stanley and Hogey?"

The light in his eyes dimmed, and he hesitated. "No, Rachael. I have heard nothing."

Why had he hesitated? The waitress arrived with my food, distracting me. My stomach rumbled. I picked up my fork and speared a bite, holding it aloft. "I'm in heaven."

Gil chuckled. "You should see your face."

"What?" I mumbled over a mouthful.

With amazing tenderness, he picked up my napkin and wiped my chin. "You be careful, Rachael Grant. I would be one unhappy papa if you got hurt."

I set down my fork. "Gil—"

He held up his hand and shook his head. "No, I still know nothing. Like five minutes ago. But I will listen. I will keep my eyes and ears open, and if I hear of anything, I will let you know." He shrugged. "Now, I must know. Why is your smile so sad?"

The weight of my worries settled on my shoulders. I

quickly told him about everything that had gone on since I'd come back to Saddle Gap. He had, of course, heard most of it already. Then I told him about Fernando.

"I don't know this Fernando you speak of. Someone like him, though, these murders, aren't his style. If he wants to mess with you, it would be ugly."

"And murder isn't ugly?"

He shrugged again. "Nah, not to a man like Fernando. They died quickly, yes?"

I nodded.

"Too easy. Fernando's type, they like to draw the pain and suffering out. Make you squirm."

A faraway look came to Gil's eyes. He stared over my shoulder, but as I had my back to the wall, I knew it wasn't plaster he studied.

"Fernando, he's the type of man to wait. Like a panther, he'll bide his time until his prey is within striking distance. He may forage out for little bites, but he is patient. He will wait to pounce until he is sure the pain he caused will linger."

His voice dropped so low I had to lay down my fork and stop eating. I felt the now-familiar shivers dance along the back of my neck. His dark eyes glistened, his expression hardened. If I hadn't known Gilbert so well, I'd fear him at this moment.

"When you least expect it, when you are most vulnerable, that's when he will strike. And not at you." His gaze focused on me. "At something precious to you, Rachael. *Someone* precious to you."

"Lauren."

He reached out and touched my forehead. The graze of his fingertip was feather soft, so light I almost thought he hadn't touched me. "Something bad is happening here. You must stop it, before more are hurt."

He shook himself, and, just as suddenly as it had come, the pall cocooning us lifted. He sprang to his feet. With a quick squeeze of my shoulder he was gone, leaving me to contemplate his warning.

Was it to beware of Fernando, or did he know something else, something he wasn't ready to share with me?

I pushed aside my plate, my appetite gone. I'm not sure how long I sat alone, staring out the window as the afternoon drifted on. When the waitress finally came to take my tray, I decided I couldn't put it off any longer. It was time to go see to my guest ranch.

Somehow, though, I didn't exactly feel like whistling "Home on the Range."

At Tumbleweeds I found a surprise waiting for me. It wasn't deserted as I'd expected; one car was pulled up at the front porch. Jamie. I went around the back and found her wrapping a rope into a ball.

"Hey, what are you doing here?" I asked.

The poor kid jumped ten feet, dropping the twine. "Rachael! Why are you here?"

I ignored the edgy tone to her voice. "Sorry. I didn't mean to scare you."

Her expression immediately softened, and she smiled and lifted the ball of twine for me to see. "I thought I'd come out here and clean up some for you, but I forgot the door would probably be locked. I think Stanley had the locks changed, too."

I tried my key and, sure enough, it didn't fit. "You're right. He did."

"Well, I guess you could break in? It's yours now, anyway."

. I nodded. "You're right. Stand back."

Using my crutch, I broke through one of the glass panes in the door. I reached through the broken pane and, like an idiot, cut my hand. "Damn!"

"Oh, no, Rachael. You hurt yourself?"

"Yes. Dammit, that hurt." I shook my hand. Little droplets of blood flickered onto the wooden deck.

Jamie shook her head, putting on a no-nonsense frown. "Now, Rachael, we can't have you bleeding all over the place. What would people think, coming up to the back door and finding this?"

I pointed to the remnants of police tape. "I think that would dissuade them from coming in first."

She laughed and, taking more care than I did, reached

through the broken glass to unfasten the lock. "Hey. It's already unlocked!" She pushed the door open. "I bet the cops forgot to lock it on their way out. Hold your hand up. Can you make it in here?"

"Sure." I glanced at the door lock. It was a simple push and twist type, easy enough to forget. I'd have to replace it with a deadbolt.

"Go to the sink and wash it off. I'll get some Band-Aids."

"Yes, ma'am!"

"Go. Now."

How she reminded me of Carmita. Another mother hen. I turned on the faucet and let the cool water trickle over my hand. A faint uneasy feeling marred the usual homey atmosphere of the main cabin. "You know, it's hard to believe this is mine now."

"I know." Jamie yanked open a cabinet and pulled out a box of bandages. "But aren't you glad?"

"Actually, I guess I might be." I turned off the faucet, and she took my hand and dabbed at the cut.

Her pale green eyes held mine for a long moment. "Lauren will be glad."

I sighed. "Jamie, I can't stay here."

With deftness born of much practice, she ripped open two Band-Aids and covered my cut. "Why not?"

"I've got a job back home, Jamie." Or at least I thought I did."

"This is your home, Rachael," she said gently. "It always has been. This is where you belong."

"Is it?" I stared out the back window. From where we stood, I could see the edge of the river where the rafts bobbed up and down at their moorings. A breeze stirred the cottonwoods, sending seed puffs flying across the yard like ethereal snowflakes. "Remember that winter, Jamie, when it snowed?"

She nodded and grinned. "Yeah. We tried to build a snowman in our front yard but had to give up. Not enough snow."

"Well, at least not enough for anything but a foot-high snowman."

"Mixed with hay." Jamie laughed as she opened one of the drawers and took out a stack of washcloths. "We had a lot of fun together, Rachael. You and me and Marshall."

I caught the wistful tone of her voice but turned away and said, "I'm going to go see if I can clean up the office."

"No!" Jamie bolted in front of me. "I mean, no, why don't you rest? You look awfully tired. I'll clean up."

"Jamie, honestly. You do way too much. You're the one who needs rest."

"I'm fine. Just go into the main hall and relax." She drew her finger through the dust left by the crime-scene investigation and held it up to show me. "This is gross. Why do they have to use so much?"

I glanced around us. The stuff was everywhere. "A little overzealous, weren't they."

She laughed. "A little. Now, go on." Jamie folded her arms across her thin chest and glared at me.

I decided then I might as well let her attack the place alone and come back later. Besides, now I had a throbbing hand to join my always-throbbing leg. "Okay, I give. I've got some stuff to do before tonight, anyway. And hey, you, thanks for the bathing suit."

Jamie's eyes lit up. "You going swimming?"

I felt myself blushing. "I still can't believe I'm going to wear that thing."

"It's not like it's a thong, Rachael." She grinned. "You'll look awesome. I promise." Somehow I doubted that. "Now scoot," she said. "Don't worry about this place. I'll have it all cleaned up before you know it. Oh, I forgot to tell you, Cathy was leaving just as I got here. She'd fed and watered the horses."

"Wonderful. Thanks, Jamie. I'm going to see her later. Maybe she'd like to help out permanently, since I'm guessing Stanley sent everyone away."

"I don't know if he did or not, Rachael. I thought he was going to just do what your granddad was doing."

I frowned as a thought zipped through my mind and then, just as quickly, disappeared. Maybe it would come later. "I'll see if the sheriff found anything at his place about his plans."

"There you go. Now scoot. Have a good time tonight. Anything else you need?"

"Just my Vicodan."

She smiled in sympathy. "You must be hurting something fierce."

I nodded. "Been popping Tylenol like candy."

"Don't worry about anything here then, okay? Just go rest."

With a semi-jaunty wave, I made my way back to Carmita's car. Unfortunately, I'd forgotten to crack the windows and it was broiling inside. I rolled all the windows down and decided, what the heck, at least I could drive around and check on the property.

My property. "Tumbleweeds," I said softly into the hot air. I could just imagine the new sign I would get to greet visitors. WELCOME TO TUMBLEWEEDS GUEST RANCH! RACHAEL GRANT, OWNER. I smiled. It actually had quite a nice ring to it.

Too bad my life was back in San Antonio. I'd have to sell the place to someone else.

Chapter 13

WITH THE CLEANUP of the guest ranch being taken care of by Jamie, I was free to run by Cathy's real quick before racing home to change for my date. I gulped. A date. A date! Why in the world, in the midst of all this chaos, was I going on a date?

"Drugs. Must be the drugs," I mumbled, though the Tylenol I'd taken that morning had worn off hours before. I sure hoped a message would be awaiting me when I got back to the cabin, letting me know my package was in. I didn't care what Malik thought—I wanted my Vicodan.

Driving back toward Saddle Gap, I passed a dusty side road I hadn't been on in years. On a sudden whim I slammed on my brakes, an awkward maneuver to perform left-footed. Turning the car around, I headed back the way I'd come, then turned onto the side road.

Visiting Cathy could wait. It'd been bugging me since arriving in Saddle Gap that I hadn't taken the time to visit my mother-in-law. Former, that is, though in my heart the petite, gray-haired woman with eyes of steel would always have a special place. I knew Marshall would probably be there tending to her, but for once I didn't care if I saw him or not. I smiled.

A few minutes later I turned beneath a chipped white iron sign shabbily announcing GRANT'S BRAHMANS, THE HOME OF CHAMPION BUSTER BROWNHORN. Buster had been Marshall's bull but was long gone now, though his progeny still wandered around a few surrounding ranches.

I felt a pang of homesickness for our brief days of happiness as I drove up on the circular drive and parked behind a bright red Jeep. I also felt a pang of sorrow at the neglected flower beds and cactus gardens, the encroachment of the surrounding wildness on what was once a prizewinning lawn. Pushing back the desert in these parts was an almost impossible task, but Emma, Marshall's mother, had been enormously gifted when it came to anything green. As my own mother had been.

Though I'd been only nine when she died, I still remembered digging in the rich Oregon dirt with her, planting pansies, impatiens, moss, and tiny, tiny violets, as we created a garden beside the waterfall my father had made. I could still remember the towering sequoia. I loved to hug trees. I remembered barely being able to reach halfway around some of the trees in our backyard.

I glanced at the cottonwood towering over Emma's house. Scraggly, ugly, and a nuisance—that was cottonwood. I suddenly wondered why I'd never gone back to Oregon, but instead thought of this harsh, hot, and demanding place as home.

I shoved the door open and nearly fell out of the car. Grabbing my crutch, I slammed the car door shut and headed for Emma's house.

The front screen door opened a crack and a blond head poked out. "Rachael?"

"Hey, just thought I'd drop by a second."

Marshall stepped out onto the porch, a frown pulling his normally staid face into a map of frustration. "Jamie's not here."

"I know. She's back at Tumbleweeds, cleaning up."

"Did you tell her you were coming?"

"I came to see Emma, Marshall. Not Jamie. Where's Lauren?"

"She's at the movies with Skipper."

"I thought Skipper was grounded."

Marshall half-smiled. "Not sure what got her into trouble, but her mom gave her a reprieve. Don't worry, though. Skipper's a good kid."

She'd better be. "Are you going to let me see Emma?"

The frown on his handsome face melted into an expression I couldn't identify. Hope? Relief? "Maybe you should come see her. She doesn't. . . ."

I pulled myself up the three steps to the porch and touched Marshall's arm. Up close, I could see the fatigue and worry in his eyes. "Marshall, what is it?"

"I don't know. She's been out of it lately, but, well, come on." He watched my slow progress, his face etched with concern. "You all right, Rachael?"

I nodded. "Just hurts. Tylenol doesn't seem to be doing the trick. And I lost my Vicodan, remember?"

"Come on. Mom's got some. You could take a couple of hers."

My eyes lit up but then I sobered. "I wish. But I imagine hers is lots stronger than mine. I called to have the prescription filled here. I just haven't had a chance to pick it up. Thanks, though."

I followed Marshall into the kitchen. Nothing much had changed here except for one remarkable thing—the absence of plants. Like outside, the greenery's surroundings had taken over, quashing the vibrancy of the rooms that made up Emma's home.

Without ivy trailing around the walls, I could see the cracks in the plaster. Several huge stone tubs, which once were home to giant ficus, held nothing but dirt. The faint scent of roses lingered in the room, though not a bloom was in sight.

As we neared the back room, the smells usually associated with a hospital took over, and for a moment I felt as if I were back in my room at San Antonio Memorial.

Marshall and Jamie had rented a huge hospital bed for Emma. She lay swaddled in a deceptively cheerful pink robe, a tattered quilt across her legs. Her hair had thinned so, the pink of her scalp showed. She stared at a picture on the wall. Only her hands indicated she was still with us. They picked restlessly at the quilt.

She turned her head to face me as I entered the room. For a moment, I thought I saw a flicker of recognition, but it passed just as quickly. Instead, she rubbed fiercely at her arms, as if brushing off ants, her motions accompanied by soft, imploring muttering.

"Mom, Rachael's here to see you."

My heart broke as Marshall gently tucked the quilt around her legs. He looked at me over his shoulder, his frustration stark and clear.

I took his cue and pulled a chair close to her and reached for her hand. "Emma, it's Rachael. I've come to see how you're doing."

She closed her pale eyes and rocked her head back and forth. Her hand felt cold to my touch. Her breathing seemed forced and heavy. Then she squeezed my hand. I stared at her for a long moment. Something didn't seem quite right. She was supposed to be dying of cancer, yet she didn't have the gauntness I expected.

She gave no outward sign of being in pain, though her bedside table hosted at least ten different bottles of medication. I picked up bottle after bottle, my consternation increasing. There were several different types of pain killers, including Vicodan. Why so many?

The squeeze of her hand had been weak, but not as weak as I'd expected, either. Emma was 64, maybe 65, and until a couple of years ago, she'd been a vibrant, energetic go-getter.

"Emma, I'll be right back."

Leaving my crutch behind, I half-hopped into the kitchen, bracing myself against the wall and furniture. Marshall sat at the table, his head cradled in his hands.

I pulled out the chair opposite him. "Marshall, we need to talk." I waited for him to compose himself.

He lifted his head and stared at me through worried eyes.

Compassion for my daughter's father made me reach for his hand. "How long has she been like this?"

He cleared his throat and looked away. "I don't know. Jamie's been taking care of her. I . . . I haven't been here much the past couple of weeks." His face flushed.

"No wonder Jamie's been so exhausted."

"What is that supposed to mean?" he snapped.

I held up my hands. "Nothing. Just that Jamie is tired, Marshall. She's been handling an awful lot by herself."

He sighed, then rubbed his face over his mouth. "I know. I'm sorry. I've been— I can't believe—" He closed his eyes and sat back, slapping his hands against his thighs. The noise cracked in the still kitchen. "Mom wasn't like this two weeks ago," he wrenched out.

"Jamie said she was doing better."

"No. No. Every night when I came home, it would be late, but I'd check on her and she'd always be asleep, so I'd go on to bed," he said, his voice hollow.

I wanted to ask him where the heck he'd been so late every night, but I kept my mouth shut and said instead, "I think she needs to go to the hospital, Marshall. Something's wrong."

"She's got cancer, Rachael."

I shook my head. "I don't think that's what's wrong." I paused, wondering how to put this. "Who's her doctor? What are all those drugs on her table?"

His head snapped back as if he were stung. "What makes you ask that?"

I scooted in my chair. "Marshall, she looks drugged."

"Some Dr. Thompson in San Angelo is her doctor."

"You've never met him?"

Marshall shook his head. "Jamie always took care of it."

"When was the last time Emma saw her doctor?"

He sank both hands into his hair and held on. He swore beneath his breath, something I rarely heard him do. "I don't know."

"Call him."

He stared at me for a moment. "Maybe we should wait until Jamie gets back."

"Call her at the ranch," I suggested. Of course, Jamie would have been the one to take her mother to the doctor. I couldn't believe, though, that Dr. Thompson would have given Emma anything to make her this lethargic.

Marshall dialed the number for Tumbleweeds and waited for a moment, then hung up. "She's not there."

I was puzzled. "She probably just stepped outside, or was vacuuming or something. Marshall, take your mother to the hospital."

Our gazes held for a moment. He finally nodded. "I'll call Skipper's mom after I get to the hospital and see if she can bring Lauren to you."

"Hurry. Call me at Mac's, okay? Or at—" I stopped, suddenly remembering my date.

"Or where?" he asked.

"Do you know Nick Rittenour?" I said, feeling awkward.

He paused for a moment, confusion in his eyes. "Nick the cop?"

I nodded. "I have a date tonight," I admitted.

"Lauren." His eyes widened.

"Don't worry about it, Marshall. Go on and take Emma to the hospital. I'll figure something out."

"I'll ask Skipper's mom if Lauren can spend the night."

"Do you think she'd mind?"

He shook his head. "I'm sure it won't be a problem." He got a plastic grocery sack and, with one sweep of his hand, pushed all the medicine bottles inside.

I touched him on the arm. "Can you handle this all right?"

"Yes, I can." He swiftly bent down and kissed me on the cheek, then grabbed my shoulders, his gaze searching mine. The look of worry and frustration was gone, replaced by determination and purpose. "Thank you. I knew something was wrong, felt it, but I wasn't sure. I've got to go." Marshall moved to his mother's side and bent to pick her up. The ease with which he cradled her in his arms tightened my throat.

I followed them outside and locked up the house. He had Emma in the front of his Jeep, buckled in, before I could get to my own car. I watched as they drove off, feeling strangely elated. It was over. Marshall and I had finally let each other go.

I just hoped and prayed it wasn't over for Emma, and that the doctors at the hospital would figure out what was really wrong.

I drove back to Tumbleweeds and parked in back, but Jamie was no longer there. I left Carmita's car still running and hobbled up the stairs to the back door. On opening it, I shook my head in amazement; the back rooms had been scrubbed clean. Jamie must have worked like a madwoman to get this done in the hour and a half I was gone.

I felt guilty for burdening her. She'd had far more pressure on her than I'd realized. Handling the responsibility of

Emma's care, when Jamie herself was so young, was too much to ask of her.

And I knew all too well that there were plenty of health professionals out there who would brush aside a young woman's worries as inconsequential. I'd encountered such people myself since I'd been injured, and nothing was more infuriating. I had the backbone to demand action; willow-like, sweet-natured Jamie did not.

Anger at Marshall for leaving so much to his sister flared anew. He should have been there with Emma and Jamie at those doctor appointments, to make sure his mother was getting proper treatment. The mixture of medications appalled me. But once again, it seemed, he'd been thinking about himself, leaving Jamie to carry that burden.

I wondered if he'd been responsible for Stanley's death—and quickly dismissed the thought. None of the people on the sheriff's list could have done it, I realized.

I also realized I was likely being pretty naive.

As I passed through the private suite that was now my own, I wiped a finger across a countertop, and it came away with nary a flick of dust. Despite the changes that had taken place, I still felt as if I were on Granddad's territory. That any minute he would come charging through the back door, insist I sit down as if I were any usual guest, and wait on me hand and foot while I watched him work.

Now this place—the land, the buildings, everything in them—was mine. It felt strange. I felt like an interloper. A thief. As I entered the office, I even looked over my shoulder, expecting to be sent packing, as I had been when I was a nosy teenager.

Instead, of course, nothing but silence accompanied me as I entered the office. Flicking on the light, I sighed in defeat. Jamie hadn't gotten that far, after all. Not only that, the place almost looked as if it had been ransacked. The Coke can was gone, so I assumed whoever had fetched it for the pathologist had been a clumsy ox. Everything on the desk had been pushed around, and half the pictures Stanley had taken off the Glory Wall were on the floor.

I pulled out Granddad's chair and sat down. For a long

moment, I did nothing but sit and let remembered sounds and impressions waft over me. They made me smile. My hand brushed across the surface of the desk, hitting the rest of the stack of photographs and sending them to the floor.

I leaned over and, with a large groan, scooped them up, plunking them back onto the desk a handful at a time. Finally I got them all, sat back up, leaned back in the chair, and gasped for breath. Damn dizzy.

After a moment I sifted through the photographs, then stopped in surprise. The photograph of me, Marshall, Pamela, and Jamie that had caught my attention in Sheriff Rosa's office was still there. I stared at the mule deer head on the wall. It stared back at me. The sheriff did have a duplicate.

When had a duplicate been made of the photograph? Where had the sheriff gotten it? I picked up the phone and called him. As he'd promised, he'd left to go fishing. I frowned, then asked for Paul Pickup.

After a quick interchange, I hung up the phone. The photograph had been found on Stanley.

It was nearly 3:45 by the time I got to the cabin. Thunderclouds had rolled back into the area, threatening to drench the town. I was in a thunderous mood myself. I wished I'd been told about the photograph from the beginning. What was the murderer trying to prove? Had he put it in Stanley's front shirt pocket, or had Stanley himself? I didn't like the implications at all.

No wonder Boone had named me as her number-one suspect, and no wonder the patrol car still waited patiently outside the cabin. Watching me—not watching out for me.

I tried to shake everything off. Nick was due to arrive at any moment, and I looked like I'd been yanked through a ringer twice. Exhaustion tugged at my limbs. My leg brace weighed two tons. And my stomach growled in protest as I pulled myself up the steps to the back door.

Despite the sultry breeze pushing against me, an unexpected shiver tickled up and down my neck and back. I glanced over my shoulder as I unlocked the door; I couldn't see the person inside the patrol car, and no one else was around.

I went inside and locked myself in. As I walked into the bathroom, I shed my clothes and my brace, turned on the shower, and stood underneath the hot stream of water.

I leaned against the shower wall and closed my eyes. The water was too hot, but I didn't care. So much had happened in the few days since I'd arrived. Stanley's death. Hogey's death. The sale of the ranch. Realizing Granddad wasn't getting any younger, and someday I was going to lose him, too. Granddad's marriage after finding love for himself, late in his own life. Realizing it was finally, truly, and irrevocably over between me and Marshall, and that I was glad.

Discovering the guest ranch was now mine.

I felt tugged a thousand different ways, emotionally and physically, but I couldn't think about what this meant to me, my future, and the life I'd built away from Saddle Gap. Though I wasn't the one responsible for finding out who killed Stanley and Hogey, I still felt the weight of their deaths on my shoulders.

And now, most of all, I was responsible for the employees of Tumbleweeds. They'd be coming back from spring hiatus, expecting a new owner, true, but they certainly wouldn't be expecting me.

I turned off the water and grabbed a towel and began to dry off. Nick would be here soon. He was probably banging on the door already, and I just couldn't hear him. I opened the bathroom door, surprised to realize I was right.

"I'm coming," I hollered.

A muffled reply came back, but it didn't sound like Nick. Puzzled, I wrapped the towel around me and, wincing the whole way, went to the front door and peered through the peephole. A short woman in a worn plaid shirt, scuffed boots, and skin-tight Wranglers stood outside, her head turned away from the door. She wore her dirty blonde hair in a ponytail tied with a length of leather.

I opened the door, and she turned around, relief etched on her face. Fat, lazy raindrops had begun to fall, and the late-afternoon breeze had picked up. It nearly blew Cathy inside.

"Rachael!" she exclaimed as I shut the door behind her.

"Thought for a sec I was gonna have to break down your door. I said to myself, 'Oh, golly, Rachael's in there, all hurt and everything, and no one in there to help her.'"

"I was in the shower. Looks like you just beat the rain."

She nodded as she walked into the room and handed me a package. "Here, this was on the front porch. Looks like a herd of cattle ran over it."

I took the sealed but crumpled brown envelope, perplexed. Ripping it open, I peered inside. My Vicodan. *Thank you, thank you, thank you.* "I guess Jamie dropped it off for me while I was gone. Hold on while I take a couple of these."

"No problem. I'll just look around a bit."

I excused myself to the kitchen for a glass of water. Malik's admonishment popped into my mind; he didn't think I needed them at all anymore. I knew he was right, as they are addictive, but right now I wanted one. Or two. I opened up the bottle and shook a couple of tablets out and frowned—they looked a little different. Must be generic. With a shrug I took one of the pills, thinking I'd take another if necessary, later.

In the living room Cathy rambled on as if I were still standing next to her. "Dang. This is nice, Rachael. I never knew this place was even here, it being tucked back here and all. And look at all these knickknacks. Must never be no little kids around here. My boys would tear this place to shreds inside five minutes."

When she finally paused for breath, I spoke. "Where are they? How are they holding up?"

"They're at their granny's. They're doing okay. I left them there so I could come to see you."

I returned to the living room and, surprising Cathy almost as much as myself, said, "I'm glad you came by. I'm sorry about Hogey, Cathy."

She said nothing as she moved from object to object, reaching out to touch, but not quite daring to. She stopped in front of one of the Monet prints. "Ain't that pretty. Hogey'd like that," she whispered. I could hear the tears in her voice as she fought for composure.

"It is beautiful, isn't it?"

"He always liked pretty things. He used to promise me, someday we'd have a place like this. And I could have all the pretty things I wanted. Once the boys'd grown up, though. You know how little boys are. Always getting into things. Getting into trouble. Just like their daddy." She wiped her eyes with the back of her hand. "Their daddy got hisself into lots of trouble, Rachael. This time I guess it got him killed."

"Cathy, I want to talk to you about Hogey. Wait and let me get dressed, okay?"

She waved her hand, still not looking at me. "Go right on ahead. I'll just stand here and admire this for a bit."

I left her and darted back into my room. I could hear her moving about the living area, finally succumbing to her desire to pick things up. I'd always liked Cathy, though her rapid-fire speech sometimes left me exhausted. I wondered what she'd seen in my slow-talking, no-good, drunk cousin. But she'd loved him fiercely—and their three babies. Now she was alone, and once again I felt a wave of compassion and, even more deeply, responsibility.

I picked up the bathing suit thing Jamie had brought me and held it up. Unbelievable. "Oh, Jamie," I muttered. My daughter wanted her parents back together—that I could understand—but Jamie clearly had her own designs. I grinned. Well, whomever I chose to wow with this outfit was my choice, not hers. I threw the bathing suit into a bag along with a cover-up, then rummaged through the closet for something suitable to wear.

I smiled in satisfaction and pulled out a brightly colored short and crop-top set. Perfect for a gloomy day. I put it on, cringing a little at the half-inch strip of skin showing between the top and the shorts. Still, I liked its tropical flair. All I needed was a lei and a drink with an umbrella in it.

I grabbed the brace out of the bathroom. Lauren had painted my toenails before we left San Antonio—they were a hot pink suitable for the occasion. I slapped on the brace and eyed myself in the mirror, then threw on some waterproof mascara and some lip gloss.

Better. Not exactly sexy, but it would do for a fun evening with friends. I picked up my comb and ran it through my hair as I hobbled back into the room.

When I walked in, Cathy was sitting on the edge of the couch, her attention focused on the Monet. I would have to see if I could get her a copy of the print. Her tears had dried.

When she saw me, she shot to her feet and grinned. "Dang, Rachael. Who you after?"

I laughed. "No one. I'm going on a date, though."

"Not Marshall, I hope."

I shot her a look. "Does everyone in this town think I'm here to see him?" I ran my comb through my hair, irritated when it became entangled in a knot.

"Not me. Besides, it's not you he's after," she said.

I rolled my eyes. "I don't care who he's after."

"You sure?"

"I'm sure, Cathy." I raised my hand as she started to protest. "No. Don't want to hear it. As long as he's happy, I don't care." Though that could explain his distraction; whoever the woman was, she was getting Marshall's almost undivided attention.

Cathy closed her mouth and shrugged. "Okay, no problem. It ain't none of my business anyway. Want me to do your hair for you? I think it's long enough for a French braid."

"Sure." I sank gratefully onto the couch and handed her my comb. "I think there's a rubber band in the kitchen drawer."

She bounded to her feet and rummaged around in the drawer, finally extricating one. She returned to the couch and, with amazing skill for a woman with all boys, began to braid my hair. "Who cut your hair for you?" she asked.

"Jamie."

"Nice color. I was thinking, now with Hogey gone, maybe I'd try some of that Nice 'n Easy stuff. He never liked the smell of none of that. Beauty parlor stink, he called it, so I never did nothing to my hair."

"Jamie could do it for you."

She paused. "Nah, I'd rather do it myself. Besides, Jamie's got enough on her platter, taking care of her ma and all. I saw her at the guest ranch, you know."

"I know. She was cleaning it up for me."

"You sure that's all? She was asking me all kinds of questions. She's kinda nosy."

I smiled. "She was just trying to help."

"Being nosy gets you into trouble. She'd better watch it. Look at what happened to my Hogey."

The snap of the rubber band pronounced her done. I turned to her and said, "Tell me what happened, Cathy."

Her face crumpled for a moment, but she took a deep breath and shook herself, as if willing the entire nightmare away. When she spoke, it was in a voice so soft I could barely hear her. "Hogey told me he saw who done Stanley in."

"What?" I fought to remain calm. "How? He wasn't anywhere near the ranch when it happened, he said."

"He lied. Oh, Rachael, you know how that boy always did like to tell a tale, but this one he kept to himself. He was done feeding the horses and was gonna head out to the feed store when it opened, but he had some time, as it was early yet, and was running a bit low on his liquor, you know? So's he knew the Conard brothers was down at the main lodge there fishing that morning, and thought he'd just run on down from the stables and talk to the boys about picking himself up a bottle or two. He didn't see them, but he did see who did it."

I tensed, preparing myself for the disappointment. "He didn't tell you who it was, did he."

"No." Cathy crumpled into the couch again, shaking her head back and forth. "No, all he told me was he parked his truck in back of some boulders. You know that big clump there, at the head of the road? No one can see the truck from there. Then he ran down the road toward Tumbleweeds. The Conard brothers were supposed to be down there fishing, real early, but he didn't want no one else to see his truck. He heard some kind of motor or something, and went around back.

"That's when he saw the murderer—the person he learned later was the murderer, as he didn't know there was a murder right then—look up straight at him. He said he got the heebie-jeebies, so he ran back up the hill to his truck."

"He didn't actually see Stanley's body, then."

"No, but when we heard about the murder we knew that he'd seen the murderer for sure. He said it was the timing.

Couldn'ta been no one else. He learned about that on 'Cops.'"

I shook my head. "The Conard brothers didn't see him, though."

"No. Not them."

I shifted on the couch and glanced at the clock. Nick was almost thirty minutes late, but I was glad. Cathy might not have told me anything if he'd been here. "Did he realize the murderer saw him?"

"I don't think so. But. . . ."

"But?"

She took a deep breath. "When he got back to his truck, he realized he'd lost his money clip. He decided to go back down and get it. It had our rent money." She stopped, her face flushed with anger. "I guess he was aiming to use it to buy more liquor, cuz our rent was past due and he still had it."

I had a feeling that happened a lot. "Go on, Cathy."

"That's when he saw a man in a red Jeep stop and talk to the brothers. They went on, and then the Jeep drove down to Tumbleweeds—"

"Wait a minute," I said. I gripped the couch, sinking my fingernails into the cushion. There were lots of Jeeps in Saddle Gap. But how many red ones? "Was the man alone?"

Cathy nodded. "Yeah, he was alone."

"Okay, go on." A pounding had started at my temples, and my chest began to hurt. I realized I was holding my breath and let it out.

"So by the time Hogey got back down there, that red Jeep was in the parking lot, but it was empty. Then the man came around the corner, walking real fast. He went to the back of one of the other vehicles and looked inside, then banged his fist on the window. He yelled something, but Hogey was too far to hear him and didn't know who he was yelling at. Then the man got in the Jeep and left again."

"Who was it, Cathy? Who did Hogey see?"

She turned her head toward me. I could see the fear etched in her eyes now, the worry. "It was Marshall. And Hogey'd thought Marshall'd seen the murderer, too."

Chapter 14

ONCE I SAW CATHY OUT THE DOOR, I went into the kitchen, pulled out one of the wooden stools, and sat with a heavy thump. It couldn't have been Marshall that Hogey saw. He wouldn't have taken Lauren back out there if he'd known someone had just been murdered. But running into the Conard brothers, maybe he felt he had to go back out and make sure they didn't mess with anything. No one trusts the Conards.

Or maybe he hadn't known anyone was murdered. Apparently he'd been angry—it was very unlike Marshall to go around thumping cars. So maybe he'd argued with somebody. But whom? And why hadn't he said anything about being out at the ranch before picking up Lauren from the cabin?

A mental image of Investigator Boone's suspect list flashed in my mind. Marshall was on there in spades. He'd been acting strangely evasive. He knew how to shoot a compound bow. I dropped my head in my hand and sighed. This was crazy. If Marshall had known about the murder before he and Lauren followed the brothers back to Tumbleweeds, he would have said something. I know he would have.

I pushed myself up from the table. I felt so weak. My leg throbbed and the all-too-familiar bolts of pain skittered through my knee.

I went to the counter and looked at the Vicodan. One obviously had not been enough. I shook two out and stared at them for a long moment. I shifted and, in so doing, the familiar bolts turned into fireworks.

I clenched my teeth as I sat abruptly back on the stool. One, two, three—I counted, eyes shut tight, as the fireworks slowly sizzled out. I'd never make it through the evening like this. I washed both the pills down.

A few moments later I was looking through the front window when Nick finally arrived. He drove a car I hadn't seen before—a stately black Lincoln Town Car. I smiled. This was better than a taxi. He opened his car door and got out. I gripped the table with both hands and stared.

It wasn't fair. He looked fantastic. I'd only seen him dressed in scuzzy clothes, and now he was appearing in my door looking like a walking advertisement for *GQ*. He wore a light green patterned golf shirt, dark green Dockers shorts, and boat shoes without socks. He'd shaved. His unruly hair was somewhat tamed into place. I half expected his dogs to tumble out of the car, but he was alone.

"Sorry I'm late," he called by way of greeting as he walked into the house. "Brought my dad's car. Thought it would be more comfortable for you."

I started to give him a hard time for being late, but the appreciation in his eyes stopped me short.

"Ms. Grant, you look fantastic."

I could feel my cheeks heat. The corner of my mouth betrayed me and I gave in to the smile. It felt good to smile. "You look good yourself. Where you been?"

Nick walked up to me, setting down his keys on the kitchen countertop. He gave me the once-over, and I found myself gulping. Then he bent down and kissed me on the cheek. I nearly fainted as his aftershave wafted over me.

"I'm sorry," he said. "I was helping out at Jenn's this afternoon, when I got a call from the station. Boone's trying to find you and figured I'd know."

"I was out running errands."

"Wearing yourself out."

I nodded. "That, too. What does she want?"

"To come by so you can sign your statement. When the deputy brought it by Rosa's office, you had already left. Boone also has a few more questions for you. They got the test results back on Stanley."

"I know. Sheriff Rosa told me. Morphine."

He picked up a banana from the fruit bowl and peeled it all the way down, then broke it in two and offered me half.

"No, thanks."

"Have you eaten?"

"A little."

"When?"

"This afternoon."

His frown deepened. "You should take better care of yourself, Rachael."

I rubbed the back of my neck. Little prickles danced along my arms. I scratched at a particularly itchy spot. "I can take care of myself just fine."

"You sure you want to leave your house tonight? You seem a little . . . tired."

"Testy, you mean," I snapped.

I could feel my face heat. I opened up the freezer. It was empty except for two Stouffer's. Cold wafted out, snapping me in the face. I scratched the back of my neck, then my cheeks. Man, my skin felt dry.

A deep wave of exhaustion suddenly washed over me. "Maybe I should stay home," I said. "For someone who's supposed to be here to rest, I've done very little of it."

Nick moved up behind me and placed both his hands on my shoulders. His hands began to move in slow, sensual circles, rubbing away the tension, rubbing away my anger, rubbing away the itch.

"Sorry," I said. "It's been a rough day."

"No, I'm sorry. You're right, I shouldn't try to tell you what to do. I know you can take care of yourself. I was just worried about you. That's all."

I let my head fall back as he hit a particularly sensitive area. A warm, curling feeling started in the pit of my stomach. It snaked through my body as his hands worked their magic.

Oh, my, what's happening here?

"Maybe I should stay home," I said once more.

"Then again, after the great meal I have planned, and a little bit of wine, and a lot of relaxing in the hot tub, I guarantee you'll sleep well tonight."

I turned and looked up at him, into his dark, smoldering eyes. *Smoldering?* I had to laugh at myself. I never thought eyes could really smolder, but Nick's sure did. They were downright hot.

How in the world could I, only two days after renewing my acquaintance with this man, possibly be so attracted to him?

I leaned against the refrigerator, grateful for its coolness, given how hot my entire body suddenly was. If he touched me again I would puddle on the floor, and then what good would I be?

"That sounds good," I heard myself saying. I felt light-headed and woozy, but whether it was from the Vicodan on an empty stomach, my general exhausted state, or the feel of Nick's mouth suddenly nuzzling against mine, I couldn't say.

I didn't care. The only thing I knew at that moment was the faint taste of mint as Nick's kiss deepened. I felt my arms lift and wrap themselves around him, and felt every part of him as he pressed me against the refrigerator. I was shame-less—and felt a delicious wickedness at the thoughts rampaging through my mind. It took me a full minute to realize the phone was ringing off the hook.

"The phone," I mumbled.

"Don't answer it."

"It might be Lauren." I pulled out of Nick's arms, gasping for breath as I sat down on the stool and picked up the phone.

It wasn't Lauren. By the time I was done and set the phone back down, I wished I had listened to Nick. I wished I hadn't picked up the phone and learned what I did right then.

For a long moment I sat still, unwilling to move. If Lauren and I hadn't come, if we'd stayed in San Antonio, we would have been there. Asleep, unsuspecting, as Fernando's gang meted out their form of justice.

Gil was right. Secretive was not Fernando's style.

I started to shake. My vision began to waver, my head swam. My arms itched, the back of my neck itched. Inside my brace, the skin burned. I snapped my eyes shut, willing the sensation to stop. My perch on the kitchen stool was sud-denly precarious.

I'd seen a lot over the years, witnessed the bitter harsh-ness of street life and felt the hatred directed at me. A lot.

One got used to it. I'd gotten used to it, just like I'd told Nick and Jenn. But now it was directed at my daughter. Fernando wanted her dead. He couldn't reach me, so he wanted her dead. And I was helpless to stop him. The tiny chink he pushed into my armor had started its collapse, and there wasn't anything I could do about it. The sides would shore no longer.

"Rachael?"

I gulped for air. Tears began to course down my cheeks. I wiped them angrily away. I wasn't going to cry. I never cried. "I can't, I can't. . . ." Cold, so cold in the room, the air snapped with it.

I remember, once, my granddad said he'd felt the Reaper walk across his spine. It happened right before he was about to go out fishing. The chill was a warning, he believed. He heeded it. Half an hour later, when the most violent lightning storm of the decade tore across the ranch, he was tucked safely in a bathroom at Tumbleweeds. Carmita and one of the guests were stuffed in there with him. Two men lost their lives that day, two who hadn't heeded the Reaper's warning.

I'd just been warned, but I still fought it. Could I do anything but fight back?

"Tell me." Nick's hands cradled my face, his thumbs stroking the betraying tears away. He leaned down, touching his forehead against mine.

I could feel the heat from his body engulf me, caress me with tenderness. I should have felt ashamed at my lack of control. Ashamed that I couldn't handle it.

Good cops took it in. We were tough. Uncrackable. Good cops handled the worst that street life could dish out, dealt with whatever needed dealing with, and tossed the rest off their shoulders. I had successfully done so for years and years, and all of a sudden, I realized Jenn was right. I wasn't able to do it anymore. I couldn't do it anymore.

But I could compose myself—and did. "A gang leader by the name of Julio Fernando broke into my condo. Tore everything up in . . . just in Lauren's room. Left my things alone. Just Lauren's. They spray painted the walls, tore apart her clothes, defecated on her bed—"

"Damn. Rachael, what's going on? Who is this Fernando character?"

I poured out everything to Nick. I told him all about a 16-year-old boy found in the middle of a Southside street, dead from an overdose of Fernando-supplied drugs. Then, about the 14-year-old girl who, in drug-induced, mindless desperation, had slashed Dave's arm twice before we could subdue her. She survived detox and told us a horrible tale about a man she knew only as Flash, who paid kids with drugs to ensnare clean kids. She'd been one of his best.

He killed her two weeks later. There was no actual proof he was responsible, but I knew. They assigned an investigator to the case, but he was overworked and overwhelmed with far too many other cases.

It took me six more weeks, but with a lot of luck I finally found him. Of course, he shot my leg twice in the process, but God smiled on me that day, and a lucky slip sent him slamming into the curb, knocking him out. But his boys were watching, and they dragged him away, a wounded, angry tiger bent on venting revenge on me.

Nick listened, saying nothing until the last words finally tumbled out. I spoke so fast I barely took a breath. My head began to swim again, and Nick pulled me against his chest and held me. He stroked my hair, soothing me. It was an exquisite feeling.

I don't know how long we stayed there—me, half on, half off the stool; Nick, standing tucked between my legs—before a subtle shift took place. The rhythmic rise and fall of his chest quickened, and in response, my own body suddenly flared, hypersensitive to his nearness. I looked up. Our eyes met. He cradled my face once again, and I expected the second kiss we shared to be tender. Gentle.

It was anything but.

Thank heavens. I was ravenous, pulling him down to me, my body pressing intimately against his, feeling him, realizing he wanted me as much as I did him. My entire body itched for him, and I couldn't stop it. I wanted to wrap myself around him, forget everything else.

I'd never been kissed like this. Never. His hands stroked and touched me, everywhere at once, but not nearly enough. I was delirious. Drained, but starving. My imagination flew as I yanked at his shirt, pulling it out of his Dockers. I wanted to feel his bare chest beneath my hands. I almost ripped his shirt off in my eagerness.

Hormones? Ha! It was Nick Rittenour that I wanted.

"Rachael." He froze, cocked his head to the side.

"Yes," I whispered, my voice hoarse. "What's wrong?"

Lights slashed across the room. We froze in mid-grope.

Lauren.

"No." He groaned, releasing me so quickly I nearly fell off the stool. He saved me once again from falling, then scooted around the kitchen island. "Lauren?"

"Yeah."

I watched as he quickly tucked his shirt back in, then turned on the faucet. He splashed his face with water and was in the process of wiping it off when what sounded like galloping horses ran up the outside steps.

Lauren burst in, giggling at something her companion was saying. They were drenched by the rain but didn't seem to care. My eyes widened at the sight of her new friend—electric green fingernails, streaked hair, and hot pink metallic miniskirt—the girl screamed trouble. They headed straight for Lauren's room.

"Whoa, young lady."

Lauren stopped. "Oh, hi, Mom." Then her gaze fell on Nick. "Who are you?" The expression on my daughter's face took me by surprise.

Lauren's companion, however, did exactly what I wanted to do. She smacked her on her back. "Gee whiz, Lauren. That's Nick Rittenour." She drew out his name with such eloquence, I had to bite my tongue. The teenager fluttered her eyelashes at Nick and sauntered toward him, extending her over-manicured hand. "Hi, Mr. Rittenour."

He nodded and shook her hand. How he managed to keep a straight face, I didn't know. "Hello, Skipper. Haven't seen you at the station in a while."

Skipper rolled her eyes dramatically. "My daddy won't let

me come down there anymore. Says I might get tossed into the slammer by mistake." She looked down at her apparel and then back at us again, her eyes puppy-dog sad, as if she'd suffered the worst betrayal. "He doesn't appreciate my taste in clothes."

I glanced at Nick.

"Her father's Sheriff Rosa's second-in-command," he said. To Skipper he said, "I've missed our backgammon games. Maybe we can play a couple more times before I leave?"

She grinned. "Awesome!"

I looked at Lauren. She glared at me, then back at Nick again, adopting a bored look. Clearly she wasn't as impressed with Nick as her friend was.

"We came to get my things for the night," Lauren said.

"It's all right with your mom?" I asked Skipper.

"Stepmom," Skipper corrected. "No problem. She's outside talking on the phone to someone. Want me to go get her?"

I nodded. "I'll help Lauren get her things."

"I don't need help."

"March." I went into Lauren's room. She followed reluctantly behind. I closed the door and sat on the bed and patted beside me. I grimaced as the itching began again. Must've gotten into something, I thought.

Lauren sat beside me, but not very willingly. It was time to get a few things straightened out.

"Lauren, I want you to straighten up your act."

"Mom, I'm not a little kid anymore."

"I know you're not. And that's why I'm going to tell you this. Mr. Rittenour is here tonight because I'm going out on a date with him."

It took her a second to comprehend what I'd said. She turned to me, anger flashing in her eyes. "But what about Daddy?"

"Your daddy and I are divorced, Lauren. We're not getting back together."

"I can't believe you're doing this to me."

I slapped the bed. "Now wait a minute, Lauren Elizabeth Grant. Doing what to you?"

Her lower lip trembled. "You're ruining everything. Aunt Jamie said—" She stopped and turned her head aside.

"Aunt Jamie said what?"

Her shoulders slumped. Thank heavens there was still enough of the little girl inside Lauren, eager to please. She went on. "Aunt Jamie said she thought that if I was really good and stayed out of your way, you and Daddy would get together again."

I sighed. I was going to kill Jamie for putting ideas in my daughter's head. "When did she say that?"

Lauren shrugged and picked at her coverlet. "I don't know. She just did." She looked at me, her eyes brimming with tears. "But Daddy said you weren't, either. He said it was over a long time ago. I didn't believe him. Why can't you guys get married again? I don't want to leave here, Mom."

I touched her on the shoulder. She stiffened but then relaxed as I pulled her to me. I'd had no idea before this trip she'd believed there was a real chance we were going to get back together again.

"I still have my job back home, Lauren. I haven't quit," I said as I released her.

"I know."

"Are you really so unhappy in San Antonio?"

Tears spilled from her eyes, and she nodded. "I want to stay here. I don't want you to be a cop anymore, Mom. I hate it," she added, her face screwed up in anger as it had when she was a baby.

Lauren had never said such things about my work. Yes, it was dangerous—recent events had proved that to her. Maybe it was the look on her face that prompted my next words, or the realization that I, too, had been thinking the same thing. Especially as the image of her room, described in detail by Dave, still filled my mind. "I know. I do, too."

"Isn't there any way we can stay here?"

I hesitated. I didn't think Sheriff Rosa had any ads out for new deputies, but there was always Piggly Wiggly. "Maybe, Lauren. I'll think about it. But this is between you and me, you hear?"

Lauren screamed. She rocketed into my arms, nearly

knocking me off the bed.

Skipper bounded into the room, followed by Nick and, to my surprise, Dr. Marisol Flores.

Skipper's stepmom?

"What's going on?" Nick asked, his expression dangerous.

"Nothing," I managed, over the two girls' joyful chatter. "Lauren, slow down," I practically shouted.

"Sorry, Mom. Skipper's stepmom is here. This is her."

A familiar face peeked over the two girls. "Hi, Rachael. Looks like our girls have met." She looked as if she was about to say something else, but she set her lips in a grim line and turned to Skipper. "Help Lauren get her things." She flashed me a questioning look. "You okay?"

"Fine. Tired," I said. "Let's go into the other room." We left the girls to their whispering.

I sat down on one of the kitchen chairs and was suddenly overwhelmed by the need to scratch beneath my brace. I ripped the Velcro tabs apart and attacked my skin but felt no relief.

"Did Nick tell you about the test results yet?" Marisol asked.

"We haven't had a chance to talk all day. Sheriff Rosa told me."

She nodded, then hesitated again before speaking. "We also found it in your cousin, Rachael."

"No mere coincidence," I said. Now my scalp began to itch.

Nick nodded. "In the beer Hogey was drinking. Marisol said the Coke can had a minute injection site. Stanley had just enough to knock him senseless."

Marisol pulled out a chair and sat. "But there was enough in your cousin's system to kill him three times over, Rachael. They wanted him dead, perhaps even more so than Stanley. The wounds were made after his death and were quite vicious."

I sat back in my chair and stared out the dark window, rubbing my neck with my hand. I thought about what Cathy had told me. The killer had wanted Hogey dead, all right, and had acted swiftly to put an end to his life. The person behind all this had covered his or her tracks well.

But whoever it was would make a mistake eventually, like

I believed Fernando would, in time. I'd paid a huge price for trying to bring him in, and it looked like I was going to continue to pay even more.

But that didn't deter me from my new pursuit. Stanley's and Hogey's killer wasn't going to win this game. I only wished I understood what this game was.

Marisol interrupted my musing. "Well, actually, the police have narrowed down their suspects to one, Rachael, based on what I found and other evidence Boone discovered."

I dropped my hand. "And?"

"I'm telling you this in the strictest confidence—"

"Who?"

The coroner spread her hands and shook her head. "Pamela. They arrested her about thirty minutes ago."

Arrested her? I stared at Marisol, dumbfounded. I blinked, then closed my eyes, as a strange wave of nausea made me want to toss what little I'd eaten. Pamela? The sheriff's notes came back to me.

Marisol went on. "Well, Pamela went to nursing school when she left here. Was with a hospital over in San Angelo until about six weeks ago."

Nick said, "Pamela lost something important on her shift, something serious enough to cost her a job."

"Let me guess. Morphine." I ran my hands through my hair and scratched my head, trying to combat the feeling of disorientation. "Was it ever located?"

"None of it was actually found. She quit her job anyway, then came back here. Boone believes some of that missing morphine ended up right here in Saddle Gap."

"Was she ever formally accused?"

"No," Marisol interjected.

"How long has she been back in Saddle Gap?"

"About two, three weeks," Nick said. "She's staying with her cousin. Merrilee Evans."

I looked at him in surprise. "Why not at her parents' house?"

Nick glanced at Marisol, then said to me, "You don't know?"

"Know what."

"Pamela's father committed suicide soon after you left Saddle Gap."

"Suicide?" I said. "No one told me it was suicide."

"That part was shoved under the carpet, but the rumors flew around town anyway. Her mother took off shortly afterward, sickened by all the gossip." He looked at me pointedly. "Pamela paid a hefty price for what happened."

"Good old small towns," Marisol said.

I ran my hand up and down my arm. The itch was getting worse. I refused to feel guilty, though. No way would I feel sorry for that woman. I couldn't. I scratched the back of my neck, the guilt dancing along anyway.

I knew what it was like to lose one's parents. At least my parents' deaths hadn't been like Pamela's father's. Why hadn't I ever heard that he had committed suicide?

I shifted on my seat. "Marisol, what other leads are there? Any?"

"What few there are point right to Pamela."

"Pamela couldn't have murdered Stanley. Or Hogey."

"What makes you say that?" Marisol asked.

I shook my head and slumped in the chair a little. For the first time in a long, long time, I thought back to my arrival in Saddle Gap after my parents died. Who had comforted me? Pamela, whose father often came out to treat guests at the ranch. Who had taken me under her wing at school, making sure the other students treated me right, or else she'd beat them to a pulp? Pamela.

Who taught me how to ride horses, fish for Mexican stonerollers in the river, hike over mountains and even put on makeup? Pamela. She'd been the sister I'd never had, at least until I'd caught her with Marshall. But murder? No.

"She just couldn't have done it," I said. "Boone is wrong."

Nick touched my hand, and I swiveled to face him, scratching at my arms.

Man, did I itch. I had to wonder about the soap I'd used.

"Rachael, she was picked up at Marshall's mom's house. He grimaced.

"You already knew all this? I wish you had told me at least about the arrest, Nick."

"There were other things on my mind."

Heat crept into my cheeks. Marisol's eyes immediately fixed on my face, and she raised her eyebrows. "They went to Pamela's house first with a search warrant." She paused. "They found several old bottles of morphine in her house."

"Her father was a doctor."

Marisol stood and shook her head. "That's true, but he's been gone a long time. These bottles weren't that old. And, what's more, there was a medicine bottle with your name on it."

"My name?"

Marisol nodded. "Recent prescription, too. Vicodan."

I stared at my hands. "My Vicodan was missing from my suitcase when I got here. Nick, the one that appeared miraculously inside the house."

I swallowed, realizing I was awfully thirsty in addition to being itchy. Not just itchy. The annoyance had started to flame my skin, I realized.

"She had nowhere else to turn," Nick said. "Her father was also a bow hunter."

I thought of the Glory Wall. The pictures of me and Jamie and Marshall, celebrating Marshall's hunt. A wave of disorientation passed through me. I needed to eat. Darn Vicodan. It had never affected me like this, though. I returned to the table and pulled out a chair, plunking down hard, scratching at my legs. I shook my head.

It didn't seem possible. Nick was right. Her dad was a bow hunter, too. But lots of people around here were. I scratched at my arms. They itched so bad. My back itched, my legs and my scalp. I ran my fingers through my hair and across my face.

"Rachael, you okay?" Marisol said.

I nodded, still scratching. The strange queasiness in my stomach grew stronger. "Why would she kill Stanley, though?" I managed to ask.

Marisol shifted in her chair. The scraping noise made me wince. "Maybe he overheard her planning to do something to you when you came back to town." She thumped the table, and my head resounded. "Then, he confronted her about it, or maybe even threatened to expose her, so she offed him."

I said, "Stanley didn't seem the type to do that. And besides, hardly anyone knew I was coming."

"Who did know?"

I hesitated. "Marshall. Lauren sent him an E-mail. I guess she could've found it if she was snooping around his mother's place."

"And remember what you told me about Lacey?" Nick asked.

I nodded. "Yeah. Her sister—"

"Her sister wasn't the only one ruined by Stanley and that group."

"Pamela's father," I said dully. "He was one of the courthouse partners. Like Beth."

"He lost everything. What happened between you and Marshall and her happened just before then, and—"

"And she lost everything, too." Revenge. A very good motive for murder.

Yet, despite the evidence against Pamela, it was hard for me to resolve the undeniable feeling that something didn't fit. But what was it? I rested my head in my hands and took a deep breath. I felt woozy and lightheaded, and the center of my chest ached. My skin was on fire.

Pamela. Could she have done it all? Alone? But Hogey had supposedly seen Marshall at Tumbleweeds. I hated to think Marshall would have kept quiet about seeing something important. Something that would help solve the murders. He would have said something if he'd seen something. Wouldn't he? Had I told Nick? I couldn't remember.

Maybe Marshall followed Pamela down there, and that was why he didn't tell me about it. He knew how I felt about her. Everyone did. What was going on? What was Marshall doing, dammit? I had to talk to him about something. Something, something. . . . Why couldn't I think?

"Kill Stanley to get back at me," I said, my voice thick. "Doesn't make any. No sense. No sense at all." I rested my head on my hands.

"Rachael?"

I tried to lift my head toward Marisol's voice, but it rolled heavily on my neck. I forced my eyes open—they felt like cotton. She was mouthing something, leaning toward me. A warm blur that smelled like Nick moved into my line of vision. Nick.

I tried to say something. Nothing came out. I sat up again. Pain seared my throat. My skin sizzled and cracked. I wrapped my arms around my stomach and doubled over, a sharp rap to my head the last thing I felt before fire-laced darkness swept me into its arms.

Chapter 15

"RACHAEL, HONEY, wake up."

Gentle hands pushed my hair back from my forehead. I swallowed, wincing at the fiery dryness in my throat. My stomach muscles hurt worse than after doing two hundred sit-ups. I opened my eyes to find myself looking into Carmita's and Granddad's smiling faces. The soft *beep-beep-beep* of a monitor beside the bed clued me in—I wasn't at Mac's.

"What happened?"

Nick appeared in my line of vision. With a knowing smile, Carmita and Granddad moved aside.

Nick sat on the edge of my bed and shook his head. "Rachael Grant, what are we going to do with you?"

"What's that supposed to mean?" I shifted uncomfortably. Every muscle in my torso area groaned in protest.

He put a hand on my stomach. The warmth felt wonderful. "Your Vicodan was switched. That bottle contained a high-dosage generic for Percodan, and you took way too much. You had quite a reaction."

"That was my fault," I said. "I noticed they looked different but. . . ." I shrugged. "I was stupid."

No one argued with me on that point.

"We think Pamela stole the original bottle," Nick said, "and switched it with the second."

"But I thought Jamie dropped it off for me."

He shrugged. "Pamela could've done it anytime before you got home, Rachael. Easy to switch. She was doing the same thing to Emma, after all."

"But why?" I said, incredulous. "Why would she try to kill Emma? Or me?" I coughed, wincing at the pain in my stomach. Carmita immediately picked up a glass of water and a straw and held it for me. I tried to take a long, gratifying sip, but she took it away too soon.

I shifted on the bed. "It doesn't make sense. Pamela wouldn't—" I winced.

"Your tummy is tender, Rachael. You mustn't overdo," Carmita admonished.

I nodded, falling back against the pillow, my eyes closed. I felt the straw against my lips and sucked on it greedily. The cool water soothed my throat. I opened my eyes and looked out the window. It was light outside. "What time is it? How long was I out?"

"All night, sweetheart," Granddad said.

All night. Wow. "What about Emma? How is she?"

"I just visited her," Carmita answered. "She's down the hall from you. She's still very weak, but she'll be fine."

"So we were right," I said.

Nick nodded. "You and Marshall saved Emma's life, Rachael. Another day or so, and she would've been dead. The docs think Pamela wanted it to look slow and natural. But she wanted Emma out of her way."

"But why? Emma never did anything to Pamela. Has she said anything about all this?"

Granddad sighed as he pulled up a chair and settled his long, lanky frame into the seat. "Well, Rachael, honey. Seems as she's denyin' everything. Won't confess to nothin'. Says she didn't do it."

I laid my head back into the pillow and closed my eyes.

Nick got up and kissed me briefly on the head. "I've got to go, punkin."

"*Punkin*?" I smiled faintly. "That's better than *ma'am*. Where you got to go?"

"I'll be back in a bit. I've got a few things to take care of before Monday."

"Oh. Okay."

I watched as Nick eased out of the door, closing it softly behind him. I sighed.

"Rachael, honey, now I know it's none of my business—"

"No, it's not, Granddad. But I guess that won't stop you from speaking your mind."

He chuckled. "Nick Rittenour's a good boy. Who knows what may happen if you stick around."

"He's leaving, Granddad. On Monday."

His blue eyes twinkled as he scratched his chin. "Georgia's only a plane ride away from here, Rachael. Course, you'll be busy running the guest ranch and won't have time for no such nonsense."

"I haven't said I was staying."

His eyes twinkled again. "I know you ain't said nothing yet, but—"

"I can't stay here."

"Why not?"

I stared at the door Nick had walked through. I was used to Granddad's gentle prodding to stick around Saddle Gap, but all the old arguments seemed lame to me now.

"Pamela won't be back, Rachael."

"I know. I can't believe it, Granddad. Pamela and I, well, we used to be so close."

"People change, Rachael, honey."

"Or," Carmita added, "they were never what they seemed in the first place."

The door opened and a small face peeked in. "Anybody awake?"

I grinned, feeling suddenly much better. "Jamie. Hey, come on in. Join the party."

She glided over and patted me on shoulder, frowning with mock sternness. "What have you done to yourself this time, Rachael?"

"I know, I know."

"Well," she said brightly. "I have done something for you. I cleaned out Mac's place and moved all your things."

"What? Why in the world did you do that?"

She sighed impatiently. "Rachael, the docs say you'll have to take it easy for a few days. I'll take care of you."

"You moved my things to your mom's?"

"Sure did. Front room. You'll be on your feet again in no time, especially with me and Marshall to help."

"How did you get in?"

"Oh, Marshall had your keys."

"Jamie, I don't—"

The door flew open again, pushed open by the tip of a silver cane. "Rachael, good lord, girlfriend. I brought you some chili. My best."

"Jenn, I can't believe—" I couldn't finish. My stomach groaned in protest at the thought of even one bite of Code Red. "You're mean," I whispered.

She laughed. "Don't worry, honey, I left the peppers out. It's mild enough for a baby."

Granddad immediately pried himself from the chair and directed Jenn to it. "We'd best be going on now, Rachael. Carmita and me'll be running by the ranch."

"When is everyone back?"

"On Monday. But don't worry yourself none. We'll take care of everything for you." Taking Carmita's hand, he left with a spring in his step. I wondered if he didn't really miss running things at Tumbleweeds. Maybe, but I doubted he'd admit it to me.

Jamie reached over and gave me a hug. "I've got to scoot, too. Go see Mom."

"Jamie, I'm so glad she's going to be okay."

A shadow crossed her face. "I know. It's awful, isn't it? I'll see you tomorrow when they let you out of this place." Then she was gone.

Jenn watched after her. I was surprised by the look on her face. "That girl."

"What?"

She shook her shoulders and frowned. "I don't know. If I didn't know her birthday was in January, I'd swear she was a Gemini."

"Why do you say that?"

My friend sat back in her chair and straightened her crooked legs out as best she could. "I saw her the other day, down at the courthouse, arguing with Carter . . . oh, what's his name. Monohan."

I wrinkled my nose. "I don't know who that is."

"Sleazebucket, is *what* he is. Jamie has no business with someone like Carter Monohan." Jenn settled back into her chair. "No, that's not right. Let me see. I don't think it's Monohan. But it's something like that." She waved her hands. "Whatever. I do know he's no good. Been in and out of jail a few times."

"I wonder if Marshall knows about him?"

"Don't know. I was outside the store, and she tore past without a word."

I was starting to get an uneasy feeling at the pit of my stomach. "Jamie's just been uptight lately."

"Taking care of someone dying of cancer can do that to you."

"Did anyone tell you? Emma was overmedicated. That's why she was failing. It wasn't the cancer killing her. They said it was Pamela who put the drugs there. And switched out my Vicodan, too."

Jenn shifted uncomfortably. "Pamela? Why would she do such a thing? I can't think of a single reason why she'd want to get rid of Emma. They've always been close."

"What?" I stared at Jenn. "What do you mean?"

She grimaced. "Well, I might as well tell you, though I promised Emma I never would. But seeing how you and Marshall are finally through and you've got Nick—"

"Jenn—"

She lifted one of her canes and pointed at me. "Let me finish. After the, um, incident with Pam and Marshall, and Pam's father committed suicide, Emma took her in."

"No way."

She nodded. "Everyone kinda kept it hush-hush."

"And that's why I never knew, didn't even know about the suicide?"

Jenn sighed, spreading her hands. "Marshall had moved out, of course. He and Pamela couldn't have gotten together again if they'd wanted to. The town wouldn't have let them."

"Good ol' Gappites."

Jenn laughed but quickly sobered. "You bet. They punished that girl for what happened—not Marshall, of course. Ticked Emma off but good. So she took Pamela in. Emma was the one who encouraged her to go on to nursing school."

"I can't believe this."

Jenn leaned forward, her expression earnest. "Emma paid

for her to go there, Rachael. And Pamela paid Emma back. Every dime."

"How do you know all this?"

"Because Pamela was one of my nurses when I was injured."

My eyes widened. "I didn't know that."

"And why would I tell you? Pamela was a saint." Jenn sat back in her chair, shaking her head. "So, no. She didn't hate you, she didn't hate Emma. Pamela Pianka had no reason whatsoever to try to kill either of you."

"Then who? Who, Jenn?"

"Who else was always around, who knew Stanley, and you, and Hogey? Think, Rachael. Who?"

Marshall. My brain was so muddled I hadn't made the connection. Marshall was alone with his mother when I arrived, unexpected, at the house. He'd been upset when I arrived— but at the time I thought it'd been because of his mom. Maybe he was upset because of me, because I interrupted him.

When Stanley was killed, Marshall was at the scene of the crime and never told anyone.

At the time of Hogey's death, Marshall was supposed to be with Lauren. But she was with her friends.

Marshall knew I didn't have my Vicodan.

What if Pamela didn't do it, after all? What if—

I lay back and closed my eyes. This was nuts. There had to be a reasonable explanation for all this. I had to talk to Marshall. Now. "Jenn, would you mind if I took a little nap right now?"

"Well, of course not." She stood, grabbing her canes. "I've got to get back to work anyway." She frowned. "Think about all I told you."

"I will."

"You make a decision yet about what to do with the ranch?"

"No. Though, I guess I'll have plenty of time on my hands for the next few days to think about it."

"Well. You know what I think."

I smiled. "I know."

"Take care, kiddo."

"I will."

I waited thirty minutes, willing my stomach to stop its roiling. Countless were the times I'd brought in folks straight from the streets to the hospital for the same treatment, but I'd had no idea getting your stomach pumped was such a horrible experience. They'd deserved it, I'd thought.

I no longer felt so high and mighty.

A nurse came in, took my vital signs, and murmured some encouragement. I pretended to be half asleep.

Once she was gone, I threw back the covers and eased onto the floor. A quick check of the closet revealed my crutch and the clothes I'd been wearing when Nick and Marisol brought me in.

My gun, unfortunately, wasn't there, but still at Mac's. No—thanks to Jamie, it was at Emma's. I'd left it locked up in a suitcase. Damn. I felt naked without it, but there was no helping it now. I picked up my shorts and had just about shrugged them on when the last person I expected to see strode into the room.

"Malik! Ever think of knocking?"

He ignored my half-dressed state and my protests. Good thing I'd kept on the hospital gown.

"Rachael, what in the heck do you think you're doing?"

My huge friend glared at me from his lofty height. He wore running shoes, blue jeans, and a sleeveless Gold's Gym T-shirt left over from college days. He also wore his classic don't mess-with-me therapist look.

"I'm getting dressed. What does it look like?"

"Looks like you're getting yourself into a mess of trouble, Lieutenant."

"Maybe. Now turn around, will you?"

"Get yourself back into bed, woman."

"I will not." Fine. If he wouldn't turn around, I would. I turned my back on him and began pulling off the hospital gown.

"Geez, woman, have you no modesty?"

I glanced over my shoulder. He'd turned around. "I lost that when I had Lauren." I buttoned the last of my buttons and grabbed my crutch. "Okay, you can turn around."

This time when he looked down at me, hands on his hips, I caught the gleam of curiosity. "What do you think you're doing?" he asked.

"I'm going to go talk to someone."

He pointed to the phone. "Don't you know how to use that thing?"

I sighed and shook my head. I also realized that maybe his appearance in the hospital room was a mighty good thing. "Are you busy right now, Malik?"

"I don't like that tone of voice, girl. You're up to something."

"You're a pain, you know that?"

"I know," he said. "But you love me anyway. So what gives?"

I sighed. "All right. I'll tell you, but you have to help me sneak out of here."

"Rachael, this isn't a movie. You can check yourself out any ol' time."

"But I need your wheels."

He opened the door. "You know something, I had the weirdest feeling I was supposed to come see you. Right now. I said to myself, 'Malik, get yourself over to Rachael, honey—'"

"Rachael, honey?"

"That's what everyone calls you, isn't it? So, like I was saying, I said to myself, 'Get yourself over to that hospital right now. Rachael's about to do something stupid if you don't. She needs you.'"

I laughed. "I'm glad you listened. And you're right. I do need you. Go get your car and meet me down front."

"Man, I'm gonna be sorry for this, aren't I?"

I grimaced. "I don't know. I may be, though." Once he was gone I picked up the phone and made a quick phone call, then went downstairs to await my reluctant chauffeur.

Half an hour later Malik and I stood outside Emma's house. There were no cars parked in the yard. Marshall, I knew, was at work. Jamie was at the hospital with her mother, so there wasn't much time before she came back.

Malik had his arms folded across his chest. "This is breaking and entering."

"No, it isn't." I reached out and jiggled the front door handle. It turned. "It's already open."

"No one leaves their houses unlocked anymore. Not even here."

I looked over my shoulder as I pushed open the door. "It *was* locked. I called . . . a locksmith friend of mine."

Malik grumbled as he followed after me. "I still say it's breaking and entering. What are we looking for, anyway?"

"I don't know."

I moved into the living area, holding onto my stomach. I had a feeling it was going to hurt for days.

Inside was cool and dark. Every shade was drawn. I entered the back room where Emma had been set up. Except for the lack of medicine bottles, everything was the same, though the bed was freshly made. The only sounds in the house were the steady drip of the kitchen faucet and Malik's harsh breathing.

"Nervous?" I asked him.

"This is crazy," he muttered. "You sure you don't know what we're looking for?"

I leaned against the wall below the stairs and gazed up at my friend. "No, I'm not sure. Malik, I think maybe Marshall's involved with this."

"Marshall? No way."

I shook my head. "Hogey told his wife that he saw Marshall at the guest ranch that morning, right before Stanley's body was found."

Malik whistled. "Did she tell the police that?"

"No. She's too scared to, I think."

"What about Pamela? I heard she was picked up for questioning."

"I don't know, Malik. But it doesn't seem right. Jenn told me some things about Pamela that have led me to believe she couldn't have done this." I swallowed, shaking my head again. The action made my head swim. "I know she did what she did with Marshall. . . ."

"Yeah, go on."

"I just can't see her killing anyone."

"But you can see Marshall?"

I sighed. "No. I don't know."

Malik rubbed his chin with his hand. "Why didn't you tell Sheriff Rosa all this? Or that investigator?"

"Rosa went fishing, and Boone told me to stay out of her business." I headed for the stairs, frowning at the long climb. "And because all I have is a gut feeling. That isn't enough to let a murder suspect free. I want to look in Marshall's room. See if there's anything that might link him to this mess." My stomach joined my leg in protest as I edged up the first step.

"Come on, girl. Hop on."

"What?"

"Turn around."

I chuckled as Malik waved for me to climb onto his back. "You sure about this?"

"What do you weigh? One twenty?"

Flatterer. "One thirty-five, I'll have you know. All woman."

He snorted. "More like one forty with that brace, but I bench-press that much with my pinkie. Get on."

I got onto his back, wrapping my arms around his broad chest. With incredible litheness he moved up the staircase, his muscles rippling effortlessly beneath me. It was like riding one of my granddad's horses. So much pent-up energy and power was mind-boggling. I'd taken only two breaths when we reached the top landing and Malik let me down.

"That was fun. Thanks."

He chuckled. "Now what?"

I moved past him, heading for Marshall's room. After he and I divorced, he'd stayed in the little house we'd bought. Sometime in the last year, though, he'd moved back in to care for his mom. His room was actually the master bedroom, his mom preferring the downstairs, leaving the upstairs as his and Jamie's domain.

I went into his room and stood in the middle, frowning. It was as precise as Marshall. A queen-size wooden four-poster dominated, neatly made up with plaid sheets. The hardwood floors gleamed beneath my feet, covered here and there with small braided rugs. Blue curtains covered the windows on two walls of the room.

In the corner, Marshall had a quite nice computer setup. I hobbled over and turned it on and watched it flicker to life.

I grinned, though my heart gave a tug. Lauren's face flashed up. My daughter as a screen saver.

I hated to think what she would go through if her daddy was a murderer.

I heard Malik rummaging behind me, but I ignored him. Marshall couldn't be responsible for any of this. It had to be Pamela.

Or someone else. But who? And why?

I suddenly felt like the intruder I was, prying where I had no business prying. I flipped off the computer and headed for the door, ready to leave, when Malik stopped me.

"Check this out."

I turned to see Malik holding a folder. Hobbling over to him, I took the folder and set it back on the desk. As soon as I opened it, the notes beside Marshall's name on the sheriff's list danced before my eyes. *Bankruptcy*

Inside the folder were copies of tax statements, credit card reports, and courthouse documents. Malik looked over my shoulder and whistled as I stared in disbelief at the long list of Marshall's angry creditors.

"Man," he said. "Really screwed himself up, didn't he?"

I nodded, dumbfounded. What had happened to Marshall? I sifted through the credit reports, battling the guilt over my nosiness. Immediately, though, I realized part of the situation—hospital bills, medication, equipment, home health care, a whole credit card devoted to Jamie's first year at college. I grimaced, guessing Emma didn't have any sort of medical insurance. Unfortunately, that wasn't surprising for someone like her.

A second card caught my eye. This one had Jamie's name on it. The amount of money she'd spent in one year staggered me—and she'd had a part-time job at a law firm, too. I shook my head. He'd lost his own house, which explained why he'd moved in here. He'd gone into serious debt to try to take care of his mother and his sister, sacrificing his own solvency to do so.

"Bad news, man," Malik said, moving over to the computer. "Think he'd kill over this?"

I shrugged. "I don't know. What good would it have done to

kill Stanley? Unless—" I flipped through the pages, then held up a piece of paper and handed it to Malik. "Unless he owed Stanley money, too."

Malik took the piece of paper and frowned. He glanced over the paper's edge at me and shook his head. "Marshall got himself in way deep, didn't he?" He handed me back the paper. I took it and put it back into the folder.

For some reason, Marshall had chosen to borrow ten grand from Stanley. I shuddered. That wouldn't have made a dent in the debt he owed.

"This doesn't look good," I finally said, closing the folder. I ran my hand through my sleep-tangled hair and sighed. Surely, surely, I wasn't so wrong about Marshall. Despite the damning evidence in that folder, I found it difficult to believe Marshall would stoop to murder to get himself out of trouble.

But, as I'd said to Malik, things didn't look too good for Marshall now. But why Hogey? Why kill him? "Doesn't look good at all." I slumped with exhaustion.

"This doesn't either. I didn't know Marshall was seeing Pamela."

I nearly slammed into the wall. "What? What are you talking about?"

He held up some papers he'd pulled out of the trash. They had been crumpled into little balls that he'd smoothed out. "Look."

I took one of the papers and stared at the words. "No way."

"What's that one say? This one's kinda graphic." He grinned, but my glare quelled him.

I grabbed one of the balls out of the trash. "'Marshall,'" I read. "'I'm scared. Someone was in my apartment again last night. Things were moved around, and there's some things of my father's missing, but the doors were locked. I know you don't want me to go. I don't, either, but I'm scared. I'm going to go to Houston, or maybe Dallas. I have friends there who can help me get a job. Please come with me. I love you.'"

It was signed with a simple "P" but I knew Malik was right. It was Pamela.

"So someone broke into her place," Malik said.

Pamela. Pamela and Marshall, after all these years. Now her strange behavior in the grocery store made sense. "Sounds like someone had the keys."

"Yeah, but maybe she was covering herself. You know, leaving false clues."

False clues. "Maybe you're right, Malik."

"About what?"

I grabbed his arm. "False clues. Think about it. All those clues pointing conveniently toward Pamela. I think they were put there deliberately."

"Who hated Pamela enough to point the finger at her?"

I slugged him on the arm. "Exactly." I felt myself drawn inexplicably toward Jamie's room. A thousand things tumbled through my mind. "Jamie," I whispered.

Leaving Malik in the middle of Marshall's room, I went to Jamie's room. Slowly, dreading what I feared I would find, I turned the knob and pushed the door open.

I nearly cried when I looked inside. The room was nothing like I'd imagined.

Malik moved up behind me. "Whose room is this? Lauren's?"

"No. Jamie's." Malik and I entered the spun-sugar-and-pink-frosting room. White furniture with gold trim, including a single-mattress canopy bed, dominated most of the space. At least fifteen teddy bears graced the pink-and-white-gingham bedspread. Matching curtains covered the windows. Bee Gees posters cluttered one wall. But it was the other wall that made me stare, openmouthed.

The entire wall was covered with photographs of me and Marshall and Lauren. Lauren's body, that is. The face of a much younger Jamie had been duplicated, cut out, and plastered on every one of the blown-up pictures. I stared at that face, 13-year-old Jamie, depicted again and again and again on each photograph, forcing herself into a nonexistent family. I didn't understand, though I was beginning to realize something was very, very wrong here.

"Look at this," Malik said.

"What?" I tore my gaze from the wall. "What is it?"

He grimaced and pointed at another picture of the three

of us, centered in an expensive frame over a small white shelf of books. It looked like a shrine, the row of books lined up neatly and draped with white lace. Malik had one in his hand. He handed it to me.

I read the first page. Flipped through more. "Oh, Jamie."

He'd picked up another and was reading it, shaking his head. "This is sick, Rachael. Listen to this. 'Rachael was home today! I'm so happy, she and me and Marshall are going to go to the fair. She left Lauren back in San Antonio. I hate that brat. She cries and whines, and is a horrible little sister. But that's okay. I'll get rid of her eventually."

"I never left her back in San Antonio, Malik. That's crazy."

He looked over my shoulder, his face still as stone. "I'm beginning to think *she* is."

Chapter 16

THE CHANGE IN HIS VOICE startled me. Behind my head I heard a sharp click. I turned around to find myself looking at the barrel of a gun.

My gun. Held by Jamie.

It was pointed straight at Malik.

"Why'd you bring him in here, Rachael? This is my room. You know that."

She fired.

I was too far away to react. Malik's eyes widened, his hands uselessly covering the blood pouring out of his stomach. "Rachael?" he said, then slumped to the ground.

Footsteps thumped up the stairs. "Aunt Jamie? What was that?"

Oh, God, no! "Lauren! Get out of here!"

But it was too late. Lauren's momentum carried her to the doorway. "Mommy, what are you doing here—" Then she saw Malik. Her eyes widened and she froze. Her gaze shifted toward her aunt and the gun still in her hand.

Jamie smiled. "That's better. Come here, Lauren."

"Jamie, no. Let her go."

The gun wavered in her hand, but Jamie's grip steadied. Her voice dripped with venom-laced honey. "No, I think Lauren needs to come to me, don't you sweetheart?"

The passage Malik had read from the diary slammed back into me. I studied Jamie. Her hair hung down in strings around her face; her eyes, so like my daughter's, glittered.

I'd faced down only one head case in my life, and that one ended when he'd put the gun in his mouth and fired. I didn't want that to happen here. *Oh, God, not here, not in front of Lauren.*

"I'm sorry, Mom. Jamie said you told her to pick me up—"

"It's okay, sweetheart. Don't worry about it."

Jamie's gaze swiveled back to me, and she smiled brightly. "How do you like my room?"

I swallowed. "It's lovely, Jamie." I shot Lauren a look. *Please, please, please*, I silently begged her as I turned my attention to Jamie. "Tell me about your mural."

I held my breath as Jamie's attention focused once more on me. Now I didn't dare look at Lauren. I didn't dare look at Malik, though his labored breathing brought tears to my eyes.

"I did it all by myself, Rachael," Jamie said proudly. "I got the idea from Granddad."

"From Granddad?" I wasn't about to point out that my grandfather was no relation to her.

She rolled her eyes. "Granddad's Glory Wall, silly."

"It's neat," I said. "We make a nice family, don't we, Jamie?"

"Uh-huh. Me and you and Marshall." She wrinkled her nose. "Marshall should be home soon, and I haven't fixed dinner yet. He likes it when I do that. I thought I'd make salmon cakes tonight."

"That sounds good."

"Yeah! You can help, now that you're here." She wrapped her arms around me and hugged me tight. "I'm so glad you're back from San Antonio. You were gone too long."

I tried to position myself to get the gun. Over Jamie's head, Lauren's gaze locked with mine, and she nodded, somehow reading my silent plea to get herself out of the room.

She backed out, her lithe feet propelling her silently along. I watched, tears stinging my eyes, as my baby girl reached the stairs and finally broke her gaze from mine and bolted away. I knew she'd get help, but from where? Emma's home was too far away from town.

I turned my attention back to Jamie and wrapped my arm around her. I was shocked by her thinness. "Hey, let's make some popcorn," I suggested.

"I don't want any popcorn. You know I don't like popcorn."

I tensed.

Immediately Jamie snapped away and stumbled back onto her bed, the gun pointed at me again. "You broke into my room."

"The door was open."

"No, it wasn't," she spit out. "You're lying."

"I came to see Marshall, Jamie."

"He's at work. He won't be back for a long time." The corner of her mouth lifted. "He hasn't been here much lately, but he promised he'd come home tonight. We've got work to do before he gets here." She hopped off her bed and pulled open a drawer. "Look. I saved this for you."

I stared, dumbfounded, at the outfit emerging. "My wedding dress?"

"Yes. Now that Pamela is really out of the way, you can marry Marshall again."

"What do you mean, Pamela's out of the way?"

She rolled her eyes. "Don't you know?"

"Tell me."

Jamie still had the gun clutched in her hand as she jumped onto the bed, tucking her legs beneath her. "Come and sit down, and I'll tell you all about it. You'll be so proud of me!"

I sat. I could still hear Malik's breath coming in raspy shudders. *Hang on, hang on.* My heart ached, and I prayed Jamie wouldn't realize Lauren was gone. But that was what she wanted, wasn't it?

"Okay," she said. "Remember Pamela's daddy worked with Stanley?"

Maybe it was best to play along. I hoped so. "Pamela's father was a doctor."

"No, no, no. On the courthouse. Remember? Anyway, when Marshall told me you were coming home for a while, and then I heard Pamela was coming back, I knew I had to do something. Cuz you couldn't. I really didn't think she'd come back, you know." She sighed. "I nearly screwed up there. But I took care of her." She reached out and patted my knee. "I had the papers proving Stanley swindled Pamela's dad."

"How?"

"I'll tell you in a minute. It was real easy to make him

leave Tumbleweeds to you. It was a win-win deal. He got the ranch he wanted, Granddad got his retirement money, and I promised I wouldn't tell about the way he'd ruined Pamela's dad and the other investors by bungling the court-house deal." She grinned. "So, once I was sure Granddad had his retirement money, and the will was signed, I killed Stanley."

The offhand way in which she shared this news made me sick. "What about Pamela?"

"Oh, that was easy. I needed to make sure it looked like a revenge killing, you know? Like Stanley made Pamela's dad commit suicide, so she killed him. You know that lady, Lacey, that you met at Malik's?"

"Yes, of course. How'd you know about her?"

Jamie grinned. "I knew she'd be there that day and she'd probably talk to you. Her son, Carter, hated Stanley, too. He was the one who gave me the papers proving Stanley screwed up the courthouse deal. He stole them when he broke into Stanley's house."

Carter Halloran, not Monohan, was the man Jenn had seen with Jamie that day. I had seen her with him, too.

"So Carter got the documents. . . ." I prompted.

"Uh-huh. I told him killing Stanley was the best revenge for ruining his mom and dad, but that we had to make sure somebody was blamed. So he broke in where Pamela was staying, and put your medicine there, and copies of the papers from Stanley's house."

"What about the morphine, Jamie?"

She grinned. "Pamela was a nurse, right? I got Carter to steal it from that hospital in San Angelo. It was easy to make it look like Pamela had stolen it. She was leaving anyway. It worked out great."

Oh Pamela, I thought. *The misery you went through.* She had come back here, despite having lost everything. Except Marshall. I wondered how long they'd been keeping in touch. Months? Years? I didn't think Jamie knew. I hoped not. "So you had Carter steal the morphine from where Pamela worked. And used that to kill Stanley. That way you could put the blame on Pamela, right?"

"Right! She still wanted Marshall, you know. I couldn't let that happen."

Now I knew she had no idea Marshall wanted Pamela, too.

"Hogey saw me, unfortunately. So I had to kill him too." She shook her head. "It took three or four beers, Rachael. He was a hard one to do in." She smiled brightly. "Oh, well, Cathy's better off without him anyway."

Our backs were to the open door. Behind us, I heard the faint sound of a door opening. I searched Jamie's face. She hadn't heard it. The gun had fallen into her lap as she told her tale. But I had to know something else.

"Jamie, why did you switch Emma's medications?"

She frowned and bit her lower lip. She looked much like the teenager she dreamed of being, her thin legs dangling off the side of the bed, her dress childlike. I thought back over the last few days, the explosions she'd had, and the strange reactions to my questions. All the signs of something bad going on were there, but this? I felt terrible for blaming Marshall.

Jamie's face suddenly crumpled, then creased into lines of anger. Her eyes flashed and she gripped the gun tight again. Damn.

"Because I hate her. She tried to stop me, Rachael. She said I was crazy."

"Stop you from what?"

"From being a family. She was trying to stop my family! It was easy to put the blame on Pamela for that, too." She laughed. "They caught her right here, did I tell you that?"

"How'd you get her to come here?"

She smirked. "It was easy. I sent her a note from Marshall to come. Then I called the sheriff and told him she was here."

"Jamie. Oh, Jamie," Marshall whispered from the doorway.

I froze, and Jamie looked up, adoration easing the sallowness of her face. "Marshall, darn. I didn't have time to make supper."

"What's going on here, Jamie? What happened here?"

I started to turn around as Marshall moved toward Malik, but the gun suddenly whipped up and pointed straight at me.

"Stop, or I'll shoot her, too. Don't make me do that, Marshall. It'll ruin everything."

"What— Dang it, Jamie, what have you done?"

Jamie flinched at the anger in her brother's voice. She slowly stood and pressed back against the closet door. I moved, ever so carefully, to where I could see Marshall. He glanced at me, his eyes haunted, the pain genuine. I could see it all click into place in his mind, the horror on his face grow. "Oh, Jamie," he said. "No."

"You heard me, didn't you Marshall. How I got rid of Pamela?"

"Why don't you give me that gun? Please, Jamie. Give me the gun," he pleaded.

"No. We can be a family again, Marshall. Isn't it wonderful?"

"No, honey, it isn't."

I sucked in my breath between clenched teeth. Anything could set Jamie off—didn't Marshall realize that? But then, he might be the only one to reach her. She held the gun, its tip wavering between us. It was like watching two different beings inhabit the same body, each warring with the other. Killer or preserver, which would win? She'd killed twice. Nearly killed her mother, and almost me.

"We can't be a family again," Marshall said, his voice gentle.

"Why not?" Jamie wailed. "It's what you wanted, isn't it Marshall? It's what you told me you wanted."

He sighed. "Wanting and having are two different things, Jamie. That was long ago, anyway. Rachael and I are friends. Nothing more."

"But what about all those letters? I saw them."

Marshall took a step forward. Unfortunately, he was on the wrong side of Jamie's bed. "Those weren't to Rachael, honey. Those were to Pamela."

"No."

"Pamela and I love each other. We're going to be married."

Jamie started to laugh. "You can't. She's in jail."

"No she's not, Jamie. She was released this morning."

I felt shivers dance along my spine but held myself still.

Jamie's attention was focused on Marshall now. "You're lying."

"No. There wasn't any evidence against her."

"You're lying. The cops wouldn't let her go," she hissed. "They had all the evidence. She killed Stanley. She killed Hogey."

"No, Jamie, she couldn't have. You see, both times, Pamela was with me."

Jamie's wail reverberated through the house. She swung the gun wildly from me to Marshall and back again. From the side of the bed, a teddy bear came flying toward her, its happy grin oblivious to the gravity of its mission. Jamie screamed.

I hurled myself at Jamie's gun, but a piercing pain in my leg sent me tumbling into her instead. The gun discharged and Jamie cried out, collapsing beneath me, as teddy bears tumbled from the bed on top of us.

Shouts filled the room, both in English and Spanish. Gil. He hadn't gone far after unlocking the house. Thank God. All was havoc—someone pulled me off the floor but I fought him, only vaguely aware it was Nick, as I realized the horrible truth: The bullet had struck Jamie.

I'd only wanted to stop her from shooting someone else. I hadn't wanted her to be hurt. She lay sprawled on the floor, gasping for air among the blood-spattered stuffed animals.

Nick drew me closer into his arms as Marshall kneeled beside his sister. I was filled with overwhelming sadness over how this had all come to an end.

With a calm that was terrible to witness, Marshall scooped up his sister's body and held it tight against his chest. Tears poured down his cheeks, mingling with the blood that seemed to be everywhere.

I watched, helpless, as Jamie died, cradled in her brother's arms.

I surveyed the main room at Tumbleweeds. This was where it all had begun a mere week before, I realized. Like then, the room was crowded with people, celebrating the guest ranch's new ownership.

And now here I sat once again—though in worse shape than last time—in Granddad's chair.

My chair, I corrected myself.

Cathy approached me, a can in either hand—a beer and a Vernors. "Which one you want?"

I reached for the beer but she pulled it back. "You sure you're not on no drugs, Rachael?"

I raised an eyebrow. "I'll never take anything stronger than an aspirin again. I promise you." But I chose the Vernors anyway and took a sip. Ah, heaven.

I watched, safely tucked in my chair, as my friends and family milled around, talking and laughing while my employees served food and drinks. I caught Gil's gaze, and he smiled and winked.

It was he who had tracked down Nick and alerted him that I might be in for some trouble. Heading home from Emma's house after unlocking it for me, he'd passed Jamie driving erratically in a blue Bronco. "She had a wild-eyed, crazy look" he'd told me when I asked him why passing her prompted him to make that phone call. That and he suddenly realized that the Bronco she was driving—which turned out to belong to Carter Halloran—might be the same one that had nearly hit me and Lauren in the parking lot at Tumbleweeds. Only now I knew Jamie had been trying to hit Lauren. Not me.

The front door opened. Marshall entered, followed by Pamela. They held hands. I watched, fighting back years of uncalled-for anger.

She almost immediately spied me sitting on the chair. I raised my Vernors in greeting, and she smiled, though I saw the faint tremor of her lips. The wedding was to take place in another month.

"Congratulations," I mouthed, and found I really did mean it. Her smile widened and she disappeared, tugged along after Marshall.

The faint smell of cinnamon preceded Nick as he walked toward me, carrying a plate of Carmita's finest. "As you ordered, ma'am."

"Nick, I asked you not to call me that."

He pulled up a chair. "Yes, I know." He hesitated. He was leaving for Georgia the next day, and we'd hardly had a chance to talk about it.

The revelation that Jamie had been responsible for Stanley's and Hogey's murders—and for nearly killing Emma, me, and Malik Goodnight—had rocked Saddle Gap. I'd been kept so busy fielding phone calls, trying to get the situation with the will settled, dealing with my own physical setback, and helping Lauren come to terms with what happened, that I'd hardly had the time or the energy to think past the next minute, much less to the day Nick was to leave.

There were so many questions. I was full of them, too. How could we not have known? Marshall, especially, bore the worst of it for not revealing what he'd seen that day behind Tumbleweeds. He knew Stanley and Jamie had argued, but he couldn't believe his beloved little sister was capable of murder.

Not until Lauren tumbled into his arms halfway down the road toward town and hysterically told him Jamie killed Malik.

Fortunately, Malik was tougher than everyone expected and was already at home recovering and enjoying all the dishes being dropped off at his house.

I had a kitchen full myself. Lauren and I had moved back to Mac's, at least for the time being. I wasn't ready to move into the guest ranch yet or to deal with all the changes in my life that were about to come. I felt somewhat overwhelmed, even now.

"How'd you like to go for a walk?" I asked Nick.

He smiled. "Sure, if you feel up to it."

I grabbed my crutches. I was, unfortunately, back to two again. The setback was temporary, but my hands were paying a high price once more. I shuffled like a turtle as we went out to the back porch. I glanced briefly at where Stanley had hung; no evidence remained, someone having industriously removed all evidence of bloodstains. The back window had been repaired, too.

It wasn't until after Jamie died that I learned Carter Halloran had been quite the expert at breaking into places without the use of a key. Even Gil was impressed. First Mac's, then the guest ranch, and of course where Pamela was staying.

I wish I could have blamed him for the break-in of my

apartment in San Antonio. At least, unlike Jamie, Carter was very much alive, though very much in jail for accessory to murder. I had to wonder how Lacey Halloran had taken the news. I felt sorry for her—perhaps most of all.

Granddad and a couple of his friends leaned against the porch rails, thin wisps of their celebratory cigars drifting up into the clear night sky. In unison they vacated the premises when they saw us coming, ambling down the stairs toward the river.

I had to fight the smile that threatened when, one after the other, curious glances were cast over stooped shoulders. Though our romance had barely had a chance to glimmer, folks in Saddle Gap already had me and Nick married off and, Lord help me, me pregnant again. Neither was likely to happen, but they were right about one thing.

I wanted Nick.

I leaned against the rough-hewn post and looked down toward the river. He came up behind me and, with only a little hesitation, wrapped his arms around me. I leaned against him, grateful for his warmth and his presence. My heart already ached with longing for him.

"So, you're staying here," he said softly in my ear.

I nodded. "Yes. Even if the will doesn't hold up, I've told Granddad that I'm not going back to San Antonio." I looked down at my knee. "I can't go back," I added, turning around in Nick's arms.

"Because of Fernando?"

I nodded. "But not just Fernando. He's out there, I know. I can only hope that when I don't show back up and I move out of my apartment that he'll disappear for good."

Nick's eyes glittered in the darkness. "He might not give up looking for you, you know."

I nodded. "Dave worries it'll make him even madder when I don't come back. But that's not what's keeping me here. It's everything else. Lauren. Granddad. My friends are here."

I smiled and shrugged my shoulders, then dared to lean my cheek against his chest. I closed my eyes to the sound of his heartbeat and the gentle rise and fall of his chest. "My home is here. I was just too caught up to realize everything I ever wanted was right here in Saddle Gap."

"Everything?"

I raised my head and looked up at him. "Almost everything."

His gaze searched mine for a moment, and then he nodded. I wondered what he was thinking. When it came right down to it, I had a hard time deciphering what I felt about whatever future we had together. I took a deep breath and smiled.

"Besides, they don't want me back anyway. My knee is too damaged, and I can't see myself doing a desk job. Dave pretended to be unhappy about it, but I know he isn't."

"What makes you say that?"

"Margaret lets him drive."

He grinned. "At least here you'll be too busy to get into trouble."

I narrowed my eyes at him. "Maybe."

"And there's another good thing. It's not so far to New Mexico."

"What's in New Mexico?"

"Me."

"You?"

"Yes, ma'am." He grinned and kissed me on my nose.

I looked over his shoulder; half a dozen smiling faces watched, pressed against the windows. I glared at them, but not one budged.

"I managed to call in a few favors," he said.

I pulled back a little, suspicious. "What do you mean?"

"Looks like I'll be doing my training in Artesia, New Mexico, instead of in Georgia. And I don't have to report until next week."

Before I could react, he bent down and kissed me. Our audience cheered, but I found I didn't care. I closed my eyes and enthusiastically returned Nick's kiss. After all, I could do as I wanted, right?

Tumbleweeds was mine.